# Whispers of the Heart

## *Christine Wissner*

Whispers of the Heart
Copyright © 2020 by Christine Wissner
Cover by Lyn Taylor
Formatted by Jacob Hammer
Published by Christine Wissner

Digital Edition ISBN:
Print Edition ISBN:
First Digital Publication:

First Print Publication:

# Whispers of the Heart

## Christine Wissner

*Wissnerchristine@yahoo.com*

*May good health and happiness be with you always.*
*Best Wishes*
*Christine Wissner*

# Dedications

For Gary and Linda who have been so supportive of me.

Janette who sweeps up my errors

Bobbi who is my sunshine. Without her laughter I could not survive.

And of course all my family and friends I love so dearly. You make my world a better place.

# Chapter One

*May 1, 1896*
*Lexington, Kentucky*

Anger bubbled through Mason Jackson.

"Damn lazy workers." He jerked his Morgan's reins and thundered past carriages, pedestrians and delivery wagons clogging up the thoroughfare. All his ire centered on the stone building two blocks away.

*My job will be done the way I planned or there'll be hell to pay.*

He'd worked too long and hard developing his craft to let a half-assed crew mess it up. Not today. Not ever.

Unlike his brother, a big city lawyer, he chose to be a tradesman. Twelve years of sawdust in his hair and splintered hands did not deter his ambition. Hell, he savored the smell of fine oil and lacquered wood and took pride in the beautiful furniture and sculptured doors he created. His talent raised eyebrows, and he damn well knew it.

He spurred his stallion forward at breakneck speed. Banks, stores and bustling shoppers blurred in a kaleidoscope of color, then he jerked back on the leather straps and the beast slid to a halt in front of the court house.

Leaping from the saddle, Mason dashed up the steps and ducked beneath the chain barrier. His shoulder knocked aside the "do not enter" sign and he shoved past the metal scaffolding. On a huff, he dug in his heels. Dust and wood shavings scattered from beneath his boots. His gaze swept the room. Splintered framework lay piled nearby and a musty odor filled his nostrils. "What a catastrophe."

Blood pulsated in his temples. "Where the hell is everyone?" he shouted.

A shuffling sound grabbed his attention as a heavyset man sauntered from a side room carrying a half-eaten sandwich.

"Where's Brad Collins?" Mason growled.

The man wiped his mouth on his shirtsleeve, then hollered over his shoulder. "Hey, Brad, someone's lookin' for ya."

Moments later, the young foreman, wearing a tool belt and leather apron, appeared in the doorway. "Ah, Mason," he said, stepping into the tundra, "Good to see ya."

"What the hell is this mess?" Mason ranted, pointing at the disassembled entry. "Didn't you look at my plans? You weren't supposed to rip out the whole damn wall. I can't believe this," he huffed, shoving his hands into the air.

"You said take out the old wood so we could install the replacement doors."

"I said make way for the new panels. Not tear out the whole damn thing." He snatched up the blueprints and rolled the parchment out on a work table. Sawdust and wood chips scattered onto the floor. "Look at this," he shouted, poking his finger in the middle of the sketches. "It shows exactly what to do. Do you see anything about removing this wall? Good God, man, what're you thinking?"

"No, sir, I-I," Collins stammered, his Adams apple bobbing like a fishing cork. "I just thought …"

Mason slammed his fist atop the blueprint Interrupting Brad's words. "Right here," he yelled, driving his index finger into the paper. "This… this is what I want. Follow my instructions." Inhaling, he reared back. "If my partner hadn't come by yesterday I'd 've never known. I had to stop what I was doing to come get this matter cleared up."

His glare deepened. "You've cost me a day's work."

He leaned closer. "Maybe I should deduct the cost of my time from your wages. "

Collins' face grew pale. He lowered his chin, then withered backward.

Several wide-eyed workers appeared in the doorway and concern tightened their features.

"No more mistakes," Mason said. "That set of doors will be ready in a week. I want everything completed by Wednesday. I don't care if you have to work day and night. I hired you because I was told you were the best in the business. Prove it. I won't let you destroy my reputation with poor workmanship. Now, get moving."

Mason swung around and started for the door.

*Christine Wissner*

"Mr. Jackson," Collins said, rushing up behind him. "I'm sorry,"

Jerking around, he replied, "I don't need apologies. I need results."

"Yes, sir," the foreman said, lowering his gaze. "We'll have this finished next week. I promise."

Mason nodded, then left through the construction area, each footfall less intense than the last. He raised his shoulder and chinked his head to the side, releasing the tension that gripped his neck.

A few strides later, he grabbed a handful of Midnight's mane and shoved his foot in the stirrup. He lifted. Leather creaked as he settled into the saddle and gathered the reins. Frowning, he glanced back at the building. With mistakes now corrected, he took a soothing breath, then pressed his heels against the stallion's sides and headed home.

He'd traveled only a short distance when he caught sight of a young boy at the roadside. Tears trailed down the lad's cheek. He pulled back on the reins and guided Midnight near the child. "What's wrong, son?" he asked.

The lad pointed at a nearby maple tree. "A dog chased my kitty up that tree and I can't get her down. I climbed up to get her, but I can't reach her. She'll die if I don't get her out of there."

Mason held his hand against his brow to shade the sun's glare. A small grey figure clung to a limb. He leaned over and held out an open palm. "Here, give me your hand," he said. The fair haired

*10*

boy, no more than five or six, stood and Mason grasped his wrist. With a solid grip, he lifted. Placing the child on his lap he clucked Midnight forward and steered the stallion to the base of the tree. After assessing the distance of the rescue, he stood in the stirrups, then boosted the lad up between the branches. "Now reach up and grab her," he said.

The young 'un wiped away his tears and then plucked the kitty from the limb. Giggling, he cuddled the tiny ball of fur and kissed her head.

"Where do you live, son?" Mason asked.

The boy pointed to the small cottage at the end of the street.

He reined Midnight around and took the child home. Lowering him to the ground, he asked, "What's your name?"

"Danny Collins."

Mason reared back in the saddle. *Surely this isn't my foreman's son.* "Is your father Brad Collins?"

"Yes sir."

*Oh my God. What a coincidence.* "Well, you take good care of that kitten and make sure she doesn't climb any more trees."

A smile widened Mason's lips as the lad took his treasure into the house, then he shook his head and continued home.

\* \* \*

The following day:

Squinting against the bright mid-morning sun, Mason moved

beneath the roofed stone well. On a sigh, he wiped his shirtsleeve across his brow to gather the perspiration. "Damn heat, anyway," he mumbled. He grasped the dipper and scooped water from the bucket. Two large gulps eased his parched throat. He jerked the paisley bandana from his back pocket. The ragged cloth was once his father's. A treasure he would cherish as a reminder of what a powerful heritage flowed through his veins. Smiling, he moistened the faded rag and dabbed it across his neck.

The rattle of an approaching buggy captured his attention. He narrowed his eyes.

Two strangers in an open carriage pulled to a halt. The well-dressed couple, a definite mismatch, glanced his way. The girl looked far too young to be this man's wife. Perhaps a daughter or granddaughter would be more accurate. Mason straightened his stance as the heavyset man stepped down and advanced toward him. The elderly gentleman had on brown trousers, a white shirt and a string tie. Shuffling forward, he removed his straw hat and the sun's rays bounced off his balding head.

Mason forced back a snicker as he wiped his hands on the kerchief and laid it aside. He chinked a smile and grasped the man's open hand. "Mornin'," he said with a nod.

"Name's Jones, Andrew Jones," his round cheeks tightening into balls and his mouth bowed upward. "That's my granddaughter, Jennifer," he said, directing a thumb over his shoulder. "We were told these stables are for sale. They belong to you?"

Mason's heart pounded against his ribs. He knew the day

would come when someone would buy the stable. *Damn, I haven't got used to selling the house, yet.* Now, he was in jeopardy of losing the stable, too. He'd lived here all his life. Soon everything would be gone. He swallowed back his emotion and introduced himself, then said, "No sir. I own the buildings here on the left. Crystal Falls Stables belongs to Trent Stone. He's family, though."

"Could I speak to him? I was told the place is for sale."

"Yes sir, it is, but Mr. Stone is in Colorado," Mason said. "But, I can help you, if you're interested in buying the place."

Oh, I'm interested. At the right price, of course. I just bought the estate next door from a man in New York."

"That would be my brother. He sent me a telegram day before yesterday saying he'd sold the property. I lived in that house all my life. I can't imagine living anywhere else."

"Then why'd you sell?"

"I'm alone now. Can't take care of that big place and run a business too."

"I understand, but glad you did. We love this area. Jenny and I stopped by a week ago and toured the estate. Beautiful. Just what we were hoping for." He lifted a finger and swept away a bead of perspiration trickling down his temple. "A local lawyer handled everything for us. He said you were away on business."

"Yes, I had to make a delivery to Louisville," Mason said, glancing over the man's shoulder at the lady in the carriage. Long blonde curls draped her shoulders. The glow of her cheeks matched her rose-colored dress and parasol. Petite in size, she sat erect and confident. Sophistication, wealth and intelligence oozed from her appearance. Her high-pitched chin assured him that beneath her beauty was a spoiled child. Staring straight ahead, impatience spilled from her demeanor as she twisted the parasol between her fingertips.

The spell was broken by the old man's voice.

"Looks like the place has been well cared for. I see a track out back, too," Jones said pointing a finger. "We can definitely use that. It's Jenny's horses I need to stable. Show horses, you know. Mostly Arabians. She has eight."

"We had several horses at one time. Ours were thoroughbreds. Folks came from all across the country to breed their mares to our stock. We had a stallion named Infinity that was every horseman's dream. He had strong bloodlines and they all wanted his foals."

He glanced once more at Jenny, then focused again on Jones. "Why don't you take your granddaughter inside the stable and look around while I tell my partner where I am? I'll join you shortly."

"Yes, yes, that sounds good. I'll get Jenny and we'll take a look."

Mason nodded, then headed for the workshop.

Several minutes later, he returned, his nerves pulled tight as a fiddle string as he paused at the door. He didn't want to sell the stable, but had no choice. This was no longer his property, but he loved the place. Tears welled in his eyes. He envisioned the horses and the sounds of buckets banging as they munched their morning feed. He remembered the smell of fresh-cut hay and the racket of the stable hands preparing the horses for training. So many memories he would always treasure. Time had changed everything. This was home. *No matter how hard I try, that will never change.*

On a ragged breath, he stepped inside. As he approached, the Jones girl faced him. A wisp of her hair bobbed in the breeze that drifted through the stable. The aroma of her perfume wafted the air. A smile tugged at the corner of his mouth. Beside him, she stood no taller than his shoulder, yet her presence filled the room. Her lips were full and as red as ripe cherries. A tingle surged beneath his skin. His gaze swept over her once more. A knot tightened in his throat. God, he hoped she wasn't the snobbish woman he had envisioned.

Mr. Jones eased up behind her and touched her shoulder. "Darling, this is Mason Jackson. He owns the shop across the way. He's a relative of the stables' owner."

Her blue eyes twinkled as she nodded and offer her lace gloved hand. "Nice to meet you, Mr. Jackson," she said in a firm, business-like tone.

His heart sang with delight and he swallowed to clear the expanding lump in his throat. "And you as well, ma'am."

Forcing his attention away from her beauty, he pointed out the qualities of the property. "There's well over a hundred acres of pastureland, including the training area. Quite suitable for your needs, I'm sure."

"Yes," the man said with a nod, then turned to his granddaughter. "What do you think, sweetie?"

"The stable and property are fine," she said. A searing glare lanced Mason. "I don't like it that the estate and stable are separate. Could we possibly buy your place? We can offer you a generous amount of money."

The hair rose on the back of Mason's neck. *How dare she try to push me off the only piece of this land I have.* His brows lowered. "No. I'll not consider any price. I've established my business here and I'm not moving. It's out of the question."

She jerked around to face the old man. "Perhaps we should go, grandfather. This man is going to be impossible to deal with."

"Now, Jenny. We've already bought the house and you're not going to find a stable any closer. I know this will be a bit of a walk for you," Jones said, "but it's everything you wanted."

Mason cleared his throat. "There is a short cut to the house from here. I'll show it to you, if you decide to buy the property. I'd have no problem in letting you use the path, but I definitely will not sell this strip of land."

Jenny swung around, then raised her parasol to shade her eyes. For several minutes she studied the pastureland once more. "I suppose this will do, grandfather."

The man shoved an open palm forward. "I guess you just sold us the place, young man. You can contact Mr. Stone, if you will, so we can close the deal."

Mason shook the man's hand. "Yes sir. I'll send him a telegram right away. I'd say he'll get back to you within a week."

As the Joneses started to leave, he said, "I'll make sure my partner and I have our horses out of the stable and clean the stalls as soon as the deal is closed."

"No need," Jenny said. "There are four more stalls than I need. You and your friend may use them. It'll probably be some time before I buy another horse. Feel free, for now, to leave them where they are."

He nodded. "Thank you, ma'am, I appreciate that."

At least there was a glimmer of kindness beneath that steel armor of hers.

He stuffed his fingertips into his denim pockets and sadness reappeared as they pulled away. It was a done deal. Crystal Falls Stables would no longer be a part of his life. His chin clinched tight and he headed for his office to compose a letter to Trent.

*Wonder what father would think?*

# Chapter Two

*Three weeks later*

An approaching carriage caught Mason's attention and he rushed to the shop window to take a look. Mr. Jones pulled his horse to a halt in front of the office. Mason removed his work apron and stepped into the afternoon sunlight. He chinked a smile, then greeted the man with an open palm. "Good to see you again, sir."

"Likewise," Jones said, grasping Mason's hand. He removed his hat and wiped his forehead with his kerchief. "Another hot day, isn't it?"

"Yes, sir. Stuffy, too. Like this most every summer. You never get used to it."

Jones adjusted his hat back atop his head. "Sure different than in New England. We lived near the seashore and there was always a breeze in the afternoon."

"Well, you won't find that here," Mason chuckled.

"I was going to move near my brother's place in South Carolina, but the summers are miserable across that area. He lives in Camden. Beautiful in the spring, but hotter than hell in the summer." He stuffed his handkerchief back into his hip pocket. "Enough chatter. Let's get down to business."

"Why don't we step into my office out of this heat," Mason said.

"Sounds like a good idea."

Mason directed him into the building and lifted the two front windows. "Would you care for a drink? I have a bottle of bourbon. Never been opened."

The man snickered. "So, you don't drink much?"

"No, not at all. Tried it a couple of times. It burns my throat going down, then I get light-headed. It's not for me," he admitted. Squinting an eye, he held the bottle up, "How about it? Want some?"

"Sure." Jones said. Removing his hat once more, he settled into a nearby chair. "Every man has a day when things go wrong and he turns to the bottle. You're young. Your day's a comin'. Women don't like to see a man drink, but sometimes we need a good snort to help us along."

Mason handed him the half-full glass, then backed up and rested his hip on the corner of his desk. "I got a telegram from both my brother and Mr. Stone. Each confirmed the deal had been closed on the house as well as the stable. Guess you can move in anytime. Pack helped me finish moving out the last furnishings from inside the house and yesterday we got things ready at the stable for the horses. If there's anything else you need, just let us know."

Jones upended the glass and gave a hiss. "Good stuff," he muttered. He glanced up and stared through glazed eyes. "Where'd you get this?"

"It was in a crate my father had hidden." Mason stared at the bottle for a moment, then looked back at the old man. You know, my father built everything you're getting today. This is where he met my mother. As luck would have it, he won a horse in a poker game that began his unbelievable journey. The mare was in foal and gave birth to one of the finest thoroughbreds in the country. He built an empire on the legs of that colt." Mason inhaled and adjusted his position. "I think they should be remembered in the closing of this deal. My father and his horse Infinity were special. I hope you'll continue to honor his name and maintain the property with the pride and respect they deserve."

"I assure you, I will," Jones said. He handed Mason back the glass. "And if you don't mind, I'll have another shot of bourbon."

Mason smiled, then poured the whiskey into the tumbler, making sure there was more than before."

Jones took a gulp. Raising a brow, he glanced up at Mason. "Damn, that's good," he stated through clinched teeth. He upended the glass once more. His face flashed red as the warmth of the liquor swept through his veins. On a sigh, he leaned back and his words fell silent. Moments later, as if hit by a cattle prod, he shot forward and began to speak. "Oh, yes, I wanted to ask you about your woodwork. I'm thinking of having something special made… like a sidebar. Jeb, that's my brother, has been appointed a position on the board of directors in Columbia, South Carolina. I forget what his title is, but I know it's an important one. Most politicians are big drinkers, you know. Anyway, he will be entertaining a lot of important people and I want him to have a nice piece for them to gather beside.

"Yes, I could do that," Mason said. "Just let me know what type wood you want. Cherry and oak are always nice. Whatever you decide."

"Wonderful," Jones said, scooting forward in his seat. "I'll get with you later about the wood. Also, I came to say we'll be moving in within the week and Jenny said the horses will be delivered on Tuesday. I'll be up at the house, but she'll be here to make sure everything goes as planned."

A breeze rustled the papers on the desk. Mason thrust his hand atop the small stack of invoices, then swept them up and shoved them into a side drawer. His gaze lifted and refocused on Jones. "Is there anything else I can do for you?"

"Not today," he said, stumbling to his feet. "Guess I'd better be on my way while I can still walk straight," he mumbled. "Jenny is up at the house waiting for me to help measure for new curtains. Women are never satisfied to leave things as they are. They always want something different."

Mason smirked, then stood and went to the door. "Thank you for stopping by. And give my regards to your granddaughter."

"I will, but I must warn you, she is an independent young lady. Strong-headed. Thinks she knows everything."

Mason laughed. He'd already figured that out. "Don't they all?"

The old man slapped his shoulder and stepped away.

A knot tied in his gut as he returned to his office and plopped down in the desk chair. All was gone. Only the small strip of land he refused to surrender remained in his possession. He leaned back as thoughts of the past crept into his mind. He realized his world unraveled the day his mother died. How well he remembered sitting at the dining room table staring into the steam rising from his coffee, tears blurring his vision.

His memory deepened. Burying his mother the previous day lay heavy on his mind that morning. Kathryn Jackson Stone had always been his pillar of strength. Even as a grown man, he asked her opinion to solidify his judgement.

He lowered his head and raked his fingers through his hair. Soon he would visit her grave, just as she had visited his father's. That image was imprinted in his memory and would never fade away. *Her love for father was greater than any I* know. *I hope I can have someone like that to love someday.*

Transfixed, he rubbed the rim of the porcelain cup with his fingertip, then grasped the handle and lifted the piece. *I sure didn't expect her to marry again. Then Trent Stone came into her life. He filled the loneliness that ate at her soul and he taught her how to smile again.*

Taking a ragged breath, he pressed the cup to his lips. Heavy footfalls approached from behind and he glanced over his shoulder.

"Come sit down, Trent," he said. "Want some coffee?"

"Don't mind if I do," he replied, then poured a cup of the brew. He lowered onto the chair across from Mason. "You doing all right?"

Mason nodded. "It's just hard to believe she's gone."

"I can hardly believe it myself. Sure miss her. Those years we had together were the best years of my life." He gulped a swallow of coffee, then continued. "I want you to know, I really loved your mother."

"Yes, I'm sure. Everyone loved mother…but in a different way, of course."

"She was special. The first moment I saw her I fell in love with her." Trent took another slurp of coffee, then tipped his head to the side. "So what're you going to do? I know you spoke of starting a business as a tradesman. I saw your work. You're quite good at designing furniture and carving unique doors and entryways. That takes a real skill. Never thought taking you and your friend Pack to visit Kassel's furniture factory years ago would lead to a profession. Strange how life takes a fella in a certain way and shows them their future without them even knowing. Just like my brother sending me here to buy your family stable. Why, that brought me right to Kathryn. That is fate, boy. Do what you're meant to do."

Mason nodded. "True, Pack and I have talked about opening our own shop for a long time. We both like carving thing. Just in different ways. He likes carving gun grips and rifle stocks and I like furniture and such. But, we don't know where or how to start a business."

Trent chuckled. "Why not start right here?"

"Here?" His gaze lifted. "This place isn't near town. We don't have a building or tools… and goodness knows we don't have any equipment."

"I can help with that," Trent said in a deep gravely tone. "What if I give you that new building beside the office? You can knock out the stalls and move in your equipment. Ever since my brother died leaving me the stables, I wondered what to do with the place. It's a lot of work running a thoroughbred stable. After our best stud, Infinity, died, we lost most of our business. Times change. I don't want to be tied down here anymore. I planned on selling the place, but I just hadn't got around to it."

Trent leaned back in his chair and his stare deepened. "Say I give you the new office with my apartment upstairs and that extra barn nearby. That should get you started. 'Sides, I think Kathryn would want me to do that for you. Pack can be your partner, then the two of you can go from there. Then I'll sell off the old stable and land."

"I can't let you do that."

"Why not?" Trent asked pushing forward. "You and your brother will inherit the estate. I'm sure you don't want to stay here in this big old house alone. Sell Jason your share, then move into the room above the office. Use the money you get out of the estate to buy what you need. Good Lord, boy, take advantage of this opportunity to make a future for yourself. If it doesn't work out…come to Colorado. Being married to your mother, I feel like I'm your father. No matter…you'll always have a home with me. Besides, I could use a big strappin' young man like you. I'll invest in some livestock and you can help me run the place."

Mason took a deep breath and glanced away. "I don't know. That sounds good. Right now, my life is a mess. Rachel and Pack are gone to Alabama to visit relatives. If I sell the place, she'll be out of a job. She's worked here for a number of years. I can't just kick her out."

"Maybe the new owners will hire her. If not, she'll be fine. Your mother left her enough money for her to live out the rest of her life without ever workin' another day," Trent said. "If you're not sure about what to do, come to Colorado with me. Take a break and think things through. It's beautiful country out there. Good for clearing one's mind."

"Yes, so mother told me," Mason snickered.

Trent took another swallow of his coffee, then said, "Or go to New York and stay with Jason for a while. There's plenty to do in New York, that's for sure."

"Naw, I'm not a big city person. I like it here in Kentucky. Lexington's always been my home."

Trent upended his cup, then set the empty mug on the table. Stuffing his fingers into his pocket, he pulled out his watch. "Mmm, getting late. I better get upstairs and finish packing if I'm gonna catch that three-fifteen train."

"Do you need me to drive you to the station?"

"No. I need to return the buggy I rented, but I'd be glad to catch a later train if you'd come with me. It's going to be a lonely ride home without Kathryn at my side."

Mason gave a nervous chuckle. "It's pretty lonely here without her, too."

Trent stood and stepped to Mason's side. With a pat on his shoulder he said, "Think over what I said, son. You're always welcome at my place and I'll do whatever I can to help you. All you need to do is ask."

Mason nodded. "Thanks," he mumbled, then poured more brew into his cup.

The sound of Trent's footfalls faded into the parlor and disappeared up the staircase.

The creak of the office door brought him back to reality. He jerked forward and Pack stepped inside, his husky torso nearly filling the entryway. The young man's ebony face beamed as he announced, "I'm leavin'."

"Leaving?" Mason asked, blinking away the cobwebs of his memory.

"Ya, I's headin' into town. Need anything?"

"Can't think of anything."

# Chapter Three

Tuesday evening, Mason locked the door of his shop and headed for his office. A refreshing breeze rustled the nearby trees. He glanced up as a flock of blackbirds lifted from the branches. A smile tugged at his lips. *How lucky I am to be surrounded by sounds of nature and thank God last night's thunderstorms swept away the stifling heat with a good soaking rain.*

A horse nickered.

Surprised, he glanced at the north pasture. So absorbed all day in his work, he'd forgotten the horses were to be delivered. He narrowed his eyes. In the distance, a dapple grey stallion galloped across the field. Memories of the pastures filled with thoroughbreds rushed into his mind. It seemed like yesterday.

He removed his work gloves and stepped forward. Several strides later, he reached the fencing and rested his arms on the top rail. With head and tail held high, the animal pranced about and snorted, then cautiously approached him. Smiling, he dipped his hand into his pocket and pulled out a piece of hard candy. The horse pressed closer. He held out the peppermint on an open palm.

The stallion's nostrils flared. Finally, his tender muzzle touched

Mason's fingertips and he nibbled at the candy.

"Hi, fella," he said. Gently, he raised the other hand and grasped the halter.

"Don't do that," a razor sharp voice reverberated over his shoulder. A half-second later, Jenny slapped his hand aside and the remaining chips of peppermint dropped to the ground.

Frowning, his glare cut sideways.

"I never give my horses sweets," she hissed.

"Sorry," he mumbled, trying to contain his resentment for being scolded. "My horse loves rock candy, so I always keep a few pieces in my pocket," he said. Noticing the sticky crumbs on his hand, he brushed his palm across his pant leg. For a moment, he stared at her and filtered his thoughts. There had to be a way to ease the strain with the hellion. This was not a good beginning to build coexistence on such close grounds.

He glanced back at the stallion. "He's beautiful. Proud and majestic," he said, watching her eyes for a signal he'd defused the tension. Just as he'd suspected, this young lady was determined to be in control.

She nodded. "Yes, Ibn is my finest horse. He's a handful to ride, but I love powerful animals."

*I can believe that. He's just like you. He wants to rule.*

"Ibn," he repeated, weaving calming words into their conversation. "How did you come up with such a beautiful name?"

"Ibn means "son of" in Arabic. He's the son of Azar. So I named him, Ibn Azar. We just call him Ibn. It's short and simple," she declared.

"And he looks so healthy and well groomed." Mason said as he continued manipulating her temperament.

A smile brightened her features. "They only get the best in grain and barley. I even have their hay shipped in. It's important to keep them fit and strong." A wisp of her hair crossed her cheek and she swept it aside. His gaze lowered. The pearl buttons on her top strained against the pressure of her breasts. Her beauty was well-protected by her sharp tongue. He must stay focused. He forced back his stare and his gaze met hers once more.

"Did you get all of your horses moved in?" he questioned.

She pressed her shoulder against the rail. "All but two. My jumpers will be here day after tomorrow." Her stare deepened and she straightened. "I hope you didn't mind my turning Ibn out for a while. He needed to work off some of that energy he'd stored up. He doesn't travel well."

"No, it's your place now. You do as you wish."

She ran her hand beneath the horse's long mane and patted his neck. "We'll try not to bother you. I know this narrow lane that separates my place from yours will get congested. You'll be having customers and my men will be working with my horses each day. When I ship them to show I'll need extra room for the bigger wagons to load and unload."

*Damn, it sounds like she wants to run her place and mine.* He snickered and lowered his gaze. "I'm sure everything will be fine."

The stallion jerked back and Mason released the halter.

Moments later, the animal galloped away.

Mason glanced up toward the estate. "How are things coming along with moving into the house?"

"I believe it's going to take longer than we first thought. I have new curtains ordered and we've a couple of pieces of furniture that should be in within a week or so. Grandfather said we must stay in the house we rented for at least another month. I believe we'll be moving in before then, but we'll see. Things often take longer than you expect."

"Jenny. Uh, may I call you Jenny?"

She narrowed her eyes. "I guess it would be better if we are on a first-name basis."

"Yes, after all, we are neighbors now," he said, as his grin faded. "You haven't mentioned your parents."

She lowered her gaze for a moment, then shot him a sharp glare. "My personal life should be no concern of yours. But if you must know, my mother and father passed several years ago in a riverboat accident. I now live with grandfather."

"I really do like him." Mason said, trying once again to sooth her agitation. "At least what little I know of him."

"He would give me the moon, if he could. It's hard not to take advantage of his generosity." For a long moment she studied Mason's features, then said, "I must get back inside and finish my work."

He cleared his throat. "Yes, ma'am. Have a good evening."

She nodded, then headed back inside the stable.

Mason's gaze followed her steps. *Well, that was a strange encounter. She certainly is all her grandfather said. Maybe selling them the stable wasn't such a good idea after all.* He shoved his hand into his denim pocket and pulled out the key to his office, then left the area.

\* \* \*

Once inside the stable, Jenny stopped in the shadow of the door and glanced back at Mason. She watched him make his way across the gravel road and into the office. His tall frame and broad shoulders were impressive, but unimportant. She had her horses to care for. Several minutes later, after she'd brushed down the chestnut mare, she again stopped to stare at the office building across the way. *I wonder if he is courting someone. I can't imagine a man that handsome without a lady friend.*

On a sigh, she shifted her gaze back to the interior of the building. The mare in the nearby stall poked her head over the gate and nickered. "Yes, I'm going to feed you," Jenny said, stepping over to rub the horse's forehead. "I know you've had a long journey. You must be starving. Let me find the grain and I'll get you some fresh water, too."

She picked up an empty bucket and headed for the well. Mason appeared in the doorway and she froze in her tracks. "Oh, my," she uttered, pressing her hand to her chest. "You startled me. I thought you had gone into your office."

"I did," he said stepping forward. "Then I realized I needed to feed Midnight."

Her tense stance relaxed and she glanced down at the metal bucket in her hand. "I was just on my way to fetch some water."

He held out his hand. "I'll get it for you," he said. "It gets pretty heavy when it's full."

"Yes, it does, but I'm quite capable of doing it myself. After today, my workers will be here to take care of such chores."

He took the metal container from her hand. "Uh-h," she stammered. "I-I need to find where they stored the grain."

Mason chuckled. "It's over there next to the tack room in that big barrel," he said pointing. "They delivered it yesterday. Pack and I's feed is in that old barrel next to our stalls. I figured we should keep the grain separate. Also, our hay is stacked on the north end of the loft. Just so you know."

"I appreciate that," she said, avoiding eye contact. "I'll be sure to tell my stable hand."

Mason nodded, then swung around to go after the water.

"Perhaps I should help you draw the water," she said, her voice still quivering, "I need water for the other horses, too."

" You tend to the grain," he said, grabbing another bucket. "I'll take care of the water."

A moment later, he disappeared through the doorway.

Jenny stifled a smile as he departed. She swung around and went about her chores just as she had done all her life. Each animal got a measured amount of oats and barley. Plus an equal amount of hay.

The two went through their duties without a word, then, when they finished, Mason gave his stallion a quick brushing before stepping out into the corridor. Again, purposely, he gave her an overdose of kindness. "Anything else I can help you with, ma'am" he asked, sweeping the flakes of hay off his denims.

"No, all I have to do now is bring in Ibn. I think he's had enough exercise for one day," she said, reaching for a lead rope.

"I'll open the gate for you. It can be a bit tricky at times," Mason declared, following along behind her. "My father had a special flap put on that piece because his horse learned how to open it."

"Smart horse," she said, her words spilling over her shoulder.

"Speaking of horses...where is your horse and carriage?"

Glancing back, she laughed. "I walked."

"Walked?"

"I came along the short-cut, you know, the path you showed us. Grandfather is up at the house. We brought some clothes and such to hang in the wardrobes. He said he would put things away while I came and tended the animals." She stopped in front of the pasture gate and called to the stallion. The beast lifted his head, then galloped forward.

Mason grasped the metal flap on the latch and she stepped in and hooked the lead strap on the Arab's halter. As Mason moved aside to allow them through, Pack came out the side door of the Craft Shop. Dixie, Mason's collie, aroused by the noise, came charging toward his master. "No," Mason yelled.

Sliding to a stop, the dog began to bark at the stranger. "No," he repeated, thrusting his arms up in front of Dixie.

Frightened, the stallion jerked back, then lunged forward, driving Jenny into the fence post. An instant later her head slammed against the building. Before either man could react she fell limp to the ground and Ibn galloped away.

"Oh, my God," Mason shouted.

Mason jerked aside the gate and kneeled beside her. Jenny's body lay limp alongside the building. Frantic, Mason felt her neck for a heartbeat. A strong steady beat touched his fingertips. On a sigh, he swept her up into his arms. "Pack, go open my office door. I need to get her inside. "

His friend nodded, then sprinted toward the bungalow.

Mason straightened and adjusted his grip on her limp body. Long strides carried him into his headquarters and he placed her on the leather couch.

Pack peered over his friend's shoulder.

"Get me a wet cloth," Mason ordered as he separated her hair to find the injury.

His partner rushed into the small kitchen as Mason continued to inspect the wound. The scrape oozed with blood atop a lump behind her ear.

As his fingertips touched the swollen area, she flinched and her eyes fluttered open.

"Mmm," she mumbled.

"Lay still," Mason said, gripping her shoulder. "Let's make sure you're all right before you get up."

Pack reappeared with a wet cloth and handed it to Mason. "She gonna be all right?" he asked.

Mason nodded. "I believe so. She may have a headache for a day or two, but it doesn't appear to be serious."

The nicker of a horse outside brought his attention to the window. The grey stallion trotted into view. Mason turned to Pack. "Go get her horse and put him in the stable, then lock that open gate."

"Ibn came back?" she asked, trying to raise her head.

"Yes, and you hold still," Mason said as his friend left, slamming the door shut behind him. "He'll take care of your horse. You just be quiet while I tend to that wound."

She dropped back into place.

He moved closer and pressed the cloth on the scrape.

"Ouch," she whimpered "Is it bleeding?"

"All down my arm," he said, then laughed out loud. "I'm kidding. There's a little blood, but not much. I think you'll live. It's going to be sore for a few days. That's about all." He stared at her for a moment, then asked, "Are you dizzy?"

"No, so can I get up now?'

He stood and offered her his hand.

She pulled in a deep breath, then sat up. Her gaze met his. "I'm sorry I caused you a problem."

"You need to be careful when you're at the stable alone. Bad things can happen."

"I will," she said gripping his hand and rising from the couch. "I really need to get home now. Grandfather will be wondering what became of me. If you will, please don't say anything to him about the accident. I don't want him to worry every time I come here."

"Sure thing," he replied, stepping aside. "Can you make it all right?"

"Yes, thank you." She crimped a guarded smile. "I'll go back the way I came." She glanced toward the stable.

Recognizing her concern, he said, "I'll check on the horses for you. I'm sure Pack will get the stallion bedded down and I'll lock up for the night."

"I appreciate that," she said, then started for the door. Once on the porch, she glanced back. "Thank you again for your help."

He nodded and she disappeared up the road.

# Chapter Four

*July 12, 1896*

Mason sauntered into his workshop. Pounding in Pack's work room drilled his eardrums. "Damn, Pack, what the hell are you doing?" he asked, knowing all too well that his partner could not hear him. The sound immediately sent his thoughts tumbling back to the beginning of his career as a tradesman. Trent gave him the building as he had promised, but it was up to the two of them to turn the place into a business. His gaze skimmed the walls, then he raised a brow as he remembered how much work it took to change the stable into a workshop. It seemed like yesterday when the transformation began. He lowered onto a nearby chair and visions of that day returned as clear as the water at Crystal Falls.

Repeated banging of a hammer riveted his ears as he entered the once-busy stable across from the main building. What the hell?

"Pack," he called out. "Is that you?"

His husky partner appeared from behind a nearby wall. "Mornin'," he said with a grin. "Thought I'd get started tearin' down these stalls. Lots of work ta do here 'fore we can make this into a workshop."

Mason grabbed a pair of leather work gloves from atop a nearby bench, then strolled over to his friend's side. "Did you stop by Kassel's furniture shop yesterday?"

"Yes, sir. Mr. Kassel helped me fill out the order for the tools I need. That stuff's expensive."

Mason chuckled. "I know. So was the equipment I needed. But it should last a long time unless we break a piece."

Pack nodded, then began banging on the wood slats once more.

Less than an hour into their project, James, the stable foreman, interrupted their work with a hardy hello. Both young men stopped pounding and greeted him with a smile.

"Looks like you two are making some progress," James said with a grin.

"We could make more if you'd grab a hammer and help us knock this wall out," Mason encouraged.

"Well, I guess I could help for a spell," he replied. "Got my morning chores done at the stable. Not much to do with only four thoroughbreds left. Trent's sellin' the main stable, you know."

"You gonna try ta stay on with the new owners?" Pack asked, removing his glove and scratching his nose.

"No. I talked it over with the wife and she wants to move nearer to Lexington. The baby should be here in the fall and she'd like to be close to schools and such."

"So you gonna sell your place?" Mason asked.

"I guess. It'll be hard to find someone to buy it, being's it's not on the main road. Not many people want to look at a smelly old barn all day."

"Wish I could buy it," Pack said. "I was born in dat house and my parents died there. Lots of memories. Good and bad." He took a deep breath. "I was pretty young when I moved in with Aunt Rachel, but I'd still like to own dat place. Not a time goes by when I pass that house that I don't think of my folks."

Mason pushed his palm against Pack's shoulder. "Maybe Rachel will buy it. Why don't you ask her?"

"Not sure 'bout dat," he replied shaking his head. "I think she'll want ta move back near her friends." Pack said . "It may be time we part ways. Now I'm grown, I want my own place. Don't get me wrong, I 'ppreciate all she's done for me, but I'm grown now. Time for me to start my own life. Just like you, Mason. You're gonna sell the estate and move in above the office. Our lives are changin'."

"True," Mason uttered, sinking into deep thought.

"Looks like all our lives are changing," James said with a smile. He glanced sideways. "Where's a crowbar? Let's get this damn building in shape so we can all move on. We have things to do."

Mason stepped aside for a moment, then returned with the iron bar and pitched it to James. "Thanks, we appreciate the help."

"Glad to," he said.

Mason stared at him for a long moment. "Isn't it strange…we all grew up together. Granted, you are a few years older, but here we are talking about our future and how it'll split us apart. True, Pack and I will be working together at times, but our skills will send us off in different directions. All our lives, Crystal Falls has kept us connected. Now, with the death of my mother, we will be scattered like wind-blown leaves on a fall day."

"Gosh, Mason," Pack said. "You should be a writer like your mother. That's a beautiful way of sayin' it."

"Yep," James concurred.

Mason's face flushed. "Stop it, you two. Let's get to work."

* * *

A brisk knock on the door scattered his memories. He rose to his feet and opened the door. A small man with wire rimmed glasses, wearing a brown suit, stared up at him. "You Mason Jackson?" the man asked.

"Yes sir, what can I do for you?"

The small man, no bigger than a jockey, pulled a paper from his coat pocket and shook it open. "I have a letter here from Elmer J. Barkley, the president of Barkley & Wells."

Mason's eyes widened. "Please, come in," he said, his pulse doubling in pace. He stepped aside, then closed the door behind the visitor. "I hope you don't mind the clutter. We can go to my office, if you prefer."

"No, no. I won't be long." He held up the paper. "Barkley & Wells have a chain of hotels from New York to Savannah, Georgia. Last week, Barkley was in Lexington and saw the new entry at the city courthouse. He immediately contacted me and ask that I to come to you. He would like for you to construct the doors and entry for his latest hotel in Atlanta. Not often does he send me out to contact outside help for his buildings. You should be honored."

"Yes, I'd like to see that," Mason said, plucking the paper from the man's hand. He studied the details, then turned to the visitor. "I see what they want, but there's no mention of what they're willing to pay for such a task." Mason fluttered the paper before the man's face.

The gentleman stepped back.

"How can I agree to a project without knowing what they'll pay? My time is valuable." His stare burrowed into the aging eyes of the messenger, all the while salivating in hopes of closing such a prestigious assignment.

"I'm sure the commission can be worked out between you and Mr. Barkley. My job is to bring you the offer."

"You tell Mr. Barkley I'd be happy to consider the job, but I must hear from him soon. I do have other projects that must be finished. If he expects this to be done right away I need time to get my crew together."

"Yes, sir, I understand," the man said with a nod.

A sharp pounding on the door brought both men around. Mason started forward but stopped short when the panel swung open. Jenny looked him square in the eye, then glanced at his visitor. "Is that your carriage parked in front of my stable?"

The man glanced at Mason. "Isn't that your stable across the way?" he asked.

"No, sir, she owns it now, but it doesn't have a sign saying so."

She perched her hands on top of her hips. "I need you to move that buggy right now. We have work to do and my men can't get around it. You left that rig tied to the gate to our training area." The glare in her eyes matched the strong tone of her voice. "I want it moved."

The visitor glanced at Mason, then back at Jenny. "Yes, ma'am," he uttered, his features stone cold with shock. "I-I was just about to leave." He looked up at Mason and said, "I'll have Mr. Barkley contact you." Wide-eyed, he nodded farewell, then rushed past her and out the door.

She turned to follow and Mason grabbed her by the arm. His jaw clamped tight and he yanked her back inside. A firestorm of anger swept through him. He slammed the door shut and jerked her around to face him. "Listen to me, young lady," the words all but blistered his lips, "don't ever barge into my shop like that again. You may be Queen on your side of the lane, but over here I will not allow you to intimidate anyone. Understand?"

She pulled her arm free and gave him a daggered stare. Her lips tightened and she reached for the doorknob. Mason slapped his hand against the panel above her head. He pressed his weight forward, holding her captive.

She swung around and jammed her elbow into his belly.

He barely flinched. "You aren't going anywhere until I'm finished," he growled.

On a muted whimper, she turned to face him. Tears welled in her eyes as she sucked a ragged breath. Anger brightened her cheeks and she fronted his strength with her pride. Lifting her chin, she stood ready to face the challenge.

"I don't want to fight with you, Jennifer," he said, his voice lowering into a harsh whisper. "There has to be respect between us. I understand your position, but you must realize I, too, have rights. And one of those rights is privacy. Don't push me. I'm not one of your hired hands."

Anger danced in her eyes while his huge frame towered over her. He eased back from the door.

"Are you finished?" she rasped, her words tumbled out as hard as stones.

"Yes," he said, and stepped aside.

Jenny grabbed the brass knob and stomped out, leaving the panel open behind her.

Mason stepped to the doorway. He caught a glimpse of the messenger leaving. What an opportunity that would be if he could land the job in Atlanta. This was the break he had waited for. Exposure in a large city could be just the springboard he needed to catapult his business.

Moments later, his gaze trekked to Jenny. She'd stopped at the gate next to the building. Twisting, she kicked the fence post, then leaned against the structure and buried her face in the crease of her arm. He cocked a crooked grin. She'll get over it. I could go comfort her, but best to let her settle down, rather than chance fanning the fire between them. She just needs to grow up. Lowering his gaze, he swung the door shut and went back to work.

# Chapter Five

Thunder rumbled overhead and Mason stepped to the window. What a welcome relief to the summer's sweltering heat. Several weeks without so much as a sprinkle had everyone complaining about their dying crops and pasturelands. Another boom of thunder shook the building. His eyes narrowed as he caught a glimpse of Jenny peering out the stable door. A week and a half had passed without speaking to her. Sure, he had seen her, but neither had made any attempt to stop and chat. Undoubtedly, she was still angry with him and he felt it best to keep his distance.

A flash of lightening filled the room with an instant glow. He drew a breath and pulled down the shade. His thoughts of her accompanied him as he returned to work. He remembered the day they met and how he could not keep his eyes off her. Those full red lips, so inviting, and her hair glistening in the sunlight. A breathtaking moment that remained hidden in the depths of his memory.

He plucked his carving tool from the work bench, then began to shave the sidebar for Mr. Jones' brother. A moment later, Jenny's image swept before him once more. Her hands perched high on her hips ready to do battle. He puffed a snicker. A beautiful lady with a mighty big attitude. *I guess no one ever stood up to her before.* A smile tugged at the corners of his mouth as he continued his job.

Again, a clap of thunder interrupted his work. He glanced up, then lowered the tool on his workbench. Three strides forward and he pulled the door aside. Darkness loomed overhead like a blanket of coal dust. Dashing wind whipped at his clothes while pellets of ice danced around his ankles. He held his forearm across his brow and tried to focus on the stable across the way. The image blurred through streams of rain running from the overhang. He sucked a heavy breath and backed inside the doorway. "Damn," he cursed, slamming the panel shut.

As he wiped the moisture from the front of his shirt Pack opened the adjoining door to their shop.

"Hell of a storm, isn't it?"

"Yes. I stepped out for just a minute and got drenched."

"You sho' did," he said as he moved closer. "But we needed the rain."

"No doubt," Mason said. Grabbing a worn cloth he dried his hands then tossed the rag aside. "Did I tell you I got the job in Atlanta? They want me to draw up the plans and send them to the builder. Once he approves them, I can get started."

Pack pressed his hip against the workbench. "Guess Miss Jones didn't kill the deal after all."

"No. Thank God. Think I'd about rung her neck if she had," he chuckled.

"Couldn't blame you for that." Pack straightened and stuffed his thumb and index finger into his shirt pocket and pulled out a paper. With a strange twinkle in his eyes, he handed it over. "I want you to read this," he said, his voice quivering.

The heading read, Atlanta Baptist Seminar. Mason glanced back at his friend as another clap of thunder rattled the window.

"Go on, read it," Pack insisted, fluttering his fingers toward the document.

Mason lowered his gaze and began to read aloud. Stunned, his eyes locked with Pack's once more. "You, you're going away to school." His statement was as much a question as it was an announcement."

"Yes. It's for Negro men only. Isn't that somethin'?" he puffed.

"I had no idea you was serious about an education. I know we taught you to read and do math, but how did you learn enough to go here?"

"Rose's sister was a teacher. I been learning' from her," he said, beaming. "It was her idea that I go to such a school. Never thought much of it at first. I only did it because Rose insisted."

Mason grabbed his friend's upper arm and gave it a shake. "That's wonderful, Pack. I'm proud of you." His words fell silent for a moment and his stare deepened. "But what about your carving and the business? You said the other day you had enough work piled up for the next six months."

"I know. I'm gonna finish the orders I have. I may wait until after the first of the year before I go away. Guess I'll just have to put aside the business until I get finished with school."

"Can you study your trade at that place? What you and I do is a skill, not something you need schoolin' for."

"No, I'm sure there won't be anything like that to study. This place turns out lawyers and teachers...even doctors, I guess."

"Good Lord, I can see it now...your name in big letters on the sign hanging above your shop."

"Won't be no doctor or lawyer, I'm sure. I just want to learn all I can. Be smart so I can do good and help other folks like me."

Mason smiled. "Well, I'm happy for you no matter what you study. I know you'll work hard. You're mother and father would've been proud of you... and so would my mother. She loved your family so much."

A tear glistened in Pack's eye. "Yes, she was a great lady."

Thunder rolled in the distance and Mason glanced up. "Sounds like the storm has passed. Maybe we can get some work done now."

Pack took back the letter, folded it and placed the piece in his shirt pocket. "I need to go to Atlanta in a week or so and find out what classes I can take. You know, meet the teachers and such."

"Why don't we go together? I need to take a look at where they're building the hotel and start thinking about what design I can use."

"Yes, I'd like that," his friend replied. "I've never been there before."

"I went a few times. The city is growing so fast I'm sure it has changed. No matter, I think I can still find my way around.

Besides, I would enjoy having your company. It's a long ride by horseback. That is unless you want to catch the train."

"No. Horseback will be fine."

Mason glanced at the sidebar. "I may take the wagon. I have time to get that piece ready to deliver to Mr. Jones' brother. Anyway, let's plan on going the end of next week."

His partner nodded, then returned to his shop.

\* \* \*

A few hours later, Mason locked up his shop and headed for the stable. The afternoon sunlight heated his shoulders as he dodged the puddles along the lane. Entering the building, the aroma of fresh hay filled his nostrils. Undoubtedly, a load had recently been delivered and placed in the loft. He glanced sideways as a movement caught his attention. Jenny was about to place her foot in the stirrup and he called, "Wait, I need to talk to you."

She lowered her foot to the ground and swung to face him.

"Is your grandfather up at the house?" he asked, stopping short of stepping on her toe.

"No," she replied, clutching Ibn's reins in her left hand. "He rode out about two hours ago and hasn't returned."

"Rode out? Where?"

"He went into the woods behind our land."

His brows slammed together. "Toward the falls?"

"I suppose." Her blue eyes snapped and her features tightened.

"I'm going to find him. He's probably lost. You can speak with him when we return."

"You know nothing about that area. I'll go get him. You stay here. It'll be dark soon. I don't need both of you lost." His stare deepened. "Why would he go back there?"

"If you must know, one of my workers saw smoke rising above the trees last evening. He thinks there are moonshiners making whiskey back there. Grandfather wanted to see if they were still there."

"Why didn't you tell me?" Mason's voice ratcheted up a notch. "That is my property and I'll take care of such matters."

"I asked him to go because I've had enough trouble trying to talk to you," she snapped. "Now if you'll excuse me, I need to find grandfather." Her lips seamed tight and she reached for the saddle horn.

"No," he said grasping her wrist. "If what you say is true, there could be trouble. Let me go alone. I don't want you to get hurt."

"But I must go if he's in danger," she insisted.

"Then I'll need to rescue both of you. You don't understand how violent these shiners are. For the past couple of years, this area has been ramped with damn moonshiners. Most send good people to be their runners. People you would not suspect. It's a crazy business. Ruthless villains who set up those stills overnight. Brew their white lightening for a few days, then move on to a new location as they try to keep ahead of the law. They would just as soon shoot you as look at you."

"Well, I'm not afraid of them," she stated, lifting her chin.

"Jenny, please. You have no Idea how mean they are. What's worse is if they find out you know who they are, they'll hunt you down and put a bullet in your head."

"I don't care. I'm going. He's the only family I have. I won't leave him out there to die," she said, pulling away from his grip.

He huffed a sigh, then grabbed a lead rope. "Let me get Midnight. You're not going out there alone."

She lifted and settled onto the saddle. "I'll be outside. I need to tell my foreman to lock up and go home, if we aren't back by nightfall."

"All right. I'll grab my gun and a lantern, then join you in a minute."

She slapped the grey stallion with the reins and disappeared through the doorway.

Moments later, as he bridled his horse, Pack entered the stable. "Where you going," his friend asked.

"We've got trouble. Smoke was spotted last night above the forest out back. I think we've got shiners back there. Jenny's grandfather went out looking for them."

"Why didn't they tell us," Pack asked, handing Mason the saddle blanket.

"Who knows? " He swung the saddle up on the stallion's back and tightened the girth. Dropping the stirrup into place he turned to face his friend. "If you have time, how about coming along. I can use your help. There may be trouble. Safety in numbers. Those moonshiners are mean sonofabitches when it comes to messing with their stills."

"I'll get saddled up," Pack said. "then stop by the shop and pick up my rifle. "I'll catch up with you."

"Great," he replied. "We'll stay on the main trail until you get there. Then we'll fan out. Cover more ground that way."

His partner nodded and grabbed his saddle as Mason left the building.

# Chapter Six

Mason reined the stallion along the narrow path and into the woods. The drumming beat of the horses' hooves silenced the katydids and crickets among the weeds. Leather creaked as he turned in the saddle. "Pack, you take the west side. Jenny and I'll follow the trail. If you find Mr. Jones, fire two shots. I'll do the same."

His friend nodded, then guided his horse to his left and soon disappeared.

Heavy thicket lay just ahead and briars on the blackberry bushes scraped Mason's boots as they passed. Memories of his childhood swirled in his mind. He recalled the times that he and Pack came to this very spot to gather berries. Pack's Aunt Rachel would fix the delicious fruit in a cobbler for their Sunday dinner dessert. *My how I loved those days.* The only downside was the chiggers that accompanied them home. Damn, they itched. He swore never to return. But, once the misery was gone, he was right back out there. A smile tugged at his lips and he glanced over at Jenny. "Careful, these bushes have some vicious thorns…and man-eating bugs, too," he said, with a chuckle.

She peered over her shoulder and frowned. "What kind of bugs?"

"You'll find out," he snickered, then spurred Midnight forward.

The glow of the evening sun cast golden rays between the leaves. A foreshadow of days to come with each getting shorter, gloomier and more miserable. He hated winter. His shoulders tightened and he shook off the chill that swept beneath his skin. There was no time for distraction. He refocused and kicked aside a broken limb blocking the trail.

"Listen," Jenny said, reining back her horse. "I heard something."

He swung around and stopped beside her. "You're right. I hear it, too." Leaning forward, he stood in the stirrups and narrowed his eyes. "Over there," he said, twisting, he pointed west. "Between the oak trees... I see a bay horse. It's saddled, but no rider."

"Grandfather has a bay," she stated, turning to face the designated area.

"Come on, let's go take a look," he said. Lowering back onto the saddle, he jigged Midnight's sides, and clucked the animal forward.

Several strides later, they approached the bay horse.

"That's definitely grandfather's gelding," she stated. Rising, she skimmed the surrounding undergrowth. "He has to be near here. He wouldn't just get off his horse and walk away."

"Well, the animal isn't tied. Maybe he fell off, or someone or something knocked him off. Who knows? No matter, we need to find him. It'll be dark soon."

Tears welled in her eyes. "What if he's hurt and can't get up?"

"Don't borrow trouble. We'll find him. This forest isn't so large that a man can disappear and never be seen again."

Mason grabbed the bay's reins and tied them to his saddle horn. "Let's keep looking."

She brushed the tear from her cheek and followed his lead.

Several strides later, gun shots rang out.

"There's Pack, he's found him." A heartbeat later three more shots cut through the air. "Shit, somethings wrong," he gasped, giving Midnight a nudge in the direction of the shots.

Jenny grabbed a handful of mane as her horse bolted forward in response to Mason's lead. She could barely hold on as low branches and tangled undergrowth lashed her arms and legs. Her whimpers faded into the twilight as the animals carried them deeper into the forest. Concern wrenched at her emotions.

Nearing the river, Mason glanced south. Mr. Jones lay draped across a log on the rocky shoreline.

He leaped to the ground and rushed to the bloody figure.

Jenny released a sharp gasp. "Is he alive?"

He rolled Jones over and placed his fingertips on the man's neck. A frown creased his forehead. "There's a heartbeat. Looks like he's been beaten and left to die."

"Who'd do such a thing?" She asked, scrambling to her grandfather's side.

"Most likely, the moonshiners. He probably stumbled onto

their set-up and they attacked him. They're an ornery bunch of sonsabitches. All they care about is the money their making running whiskey."

He lifted Jones and spotted two bullet holes in his chest, another in his shoulder. On a grunt, he jerked the hanky from his pant pocket and placed it beneath the blood stained shirt, then eased Jones onto his back. "He's lost a lot of blood. We need to get him home right away."

She crumpled to her knees. Whimpering, she shoved Mason aside. Cradling her grandfather's cheeks in her palms, she whispered, "I love you so much. Please don't die. I need you."

He sucked a ragged breath and his eyelids fluttered, then on a sigh, he fell limp.

"No," she pleaded, "please don't leave me."

Mason grasped her upper arms, pulling her away.

Crying out loud, she swung around and he engulfed her in his embrace. Her body quaked and she clung to him, releasing a flood of emotion. Her warmth melted into him and he nestled his chin against her neck and inhaled. The scent stirred the memory of their first meeting in the stable. He drew another breath, capturing the aroma once more, pressing her closer, the beat of her heart joining in rhythm with his.

An instant later, she pushed away.

"I-I'm sorry," she stammered, struggling to force the words through her constricted throat.

"I understand," he said. He compressed his lips and stood,

then offered his hand. "Come, let's take him home."

She nodded and, with his help, staggered to her feet.

He gathered her horse's reins and held the animal steady as she settled into the saddle.

Suddenly the pounding of galloping hooves caught his attention and he turned.

Pack waved a hand and rode up and stopped before them. "I heard the gun shots," he said. "I thought at first it was you signaling you'd found Mr. Jones, but then I heard more than two. What happened?"

"We heard them, too," Mason declared, "Found his horse a way's from here and that's when we heard the shots. Not sure how he got here. He must've run into the shiners. Maybe they caught him and beat him and the animal ran away. Guess they shot him so he couldn't identify them. Anyway, when we got here, we found him like this. All I know is, there'll be hell to pay for this."

"No doubt," Pack said, reining his horse alongside Mason. "Well, now they're going to really be mad. I found their stills. I was knocking them down when I heard the shots." He glanced over at Jones. "He dead?"

"Yep, we're taking him back to the house."

Pack glanced over at Jenny. "Sorry, ma'am, for your loss."

"Thank you," she muttered, straightening in the saddle, regaining her composure.

He slipped from his horse and joined Mason, then lifted the old man and placed him, face down, across the bay.

"Do you have to take him back like that? It looks so hard-hearted."

"We can leave him here until tomorrow and pick him up with a wagon, if you prefer," Mason said. "Don't know what we'll find when we return. Lots of hungry wild animals around here. They don't much care if it's man or beast. To them, it's just an easy meal."

She squeezed her eyes tight and turned away. "Never mind," she muttered.

Mason gathered the rope from his saddle and secured Jones in place, then stepped back. "There, that should do." He glanced at Pack. "Let's get going before those bastards decide to come back."

# Chapter Seven

*Three hours later*

Mason swung open the front door, then turned to face Jenny. "You sure you'll be all right?"

"I appreciate you bringing grandfather home and please thank Pack, as well. I'm afraid I haven't shown very good manners tonight."

"We understand," he said. "Do you need me to fetch the undertaker tomorrow?"

"No, I'm quite capable of making all the arrangements. I think I'll have a private service. I'll ask the minister to say a few words. We've only attended the church a few times since we moved in, but I'm sure he'll do that for me. There's no family or close friends nearby so I'll keep it simple. When it's over I'll send his body back to New England and have him buried beside grandmother."

He looked into her swollen eyes. "What about your uncle? The one in South Carolina. Shouldn't you let him know?"

"I'll send him a wire when I'm in town tomorrow," she said and glanced at the staircase, then back at him. "Now if you don't mind, I'm exhausted. I really do need to go up to bed."

"Sure. I have to do a couple of things at the shop, then I'll be at my place. Come get me if you need anything,"

She nodded and turned toward the stairs. A heartbeat later, a gun fired and glass shattered across Mason's arm and chest.

"Get down," he yelled, diving to the floor.

Jenny screamed and ducked behind a nearby leather chair.

Another crack of gunfire and the parlor window exploded, sending slivers of glass into the curtain and across the room.

Mason kicked the front door shut and scooted the hall table in front of the door. Wide-eyed, he scanned the foyer in search of something to use in defense. His rifle was of no use, he left it in the sheath on his saddle.

He glanced at Jenny, "I need a gun," he shouted. "Did your grandfather keep one here in the house?"

"Y-Yes," she said, her voice quivering. "I-I'll go get it."

"No, you stay there; just tell me where it is."

"In that small closet beneath the staircase."

He looked down at the blood on his hand and shirtsleeve. The front of his shirt was riddled with holes and dotted with blood. Grimacing, he pulled a sliver of glass from between his knuckles and wrapped his hand with his handkerchief. The other wounds would have to wait. He lowered on his knees and crawled across the parlor floor to the small storage beneath the steps. On a jerk, he opened the door and grabbed the shotgun.

He slammed the panel closed and, at the same time, a pounding fist rattled the front door. Mason cocked the shotgun, then Pack called his name.

Surprised, Mason eased his finger off the trigger.

"Open up," his friend yelled.

Mason hustled to his feet and shoved the hall table aside, then jerked open the door. In the dim light he saw two figures standing on the porch. Pack stood with his gun against the side of a young man's head and held the back of his shirt with a tight grip. "Get in there," Pack growled, "before I blow your brains out"

The young man lowered his chin and shuffled into the foyer, stopping amidst the shattered glass.

"Who's this?" Mason asked, stepping in front of the stranger.

"Not sure if it's a burglar or some idiot with a gun shooting out windows. I heard the shots. That's why I came. All I know is he was running down the lane toward the main road. He practically ran into my arms. Guess he didn't see me in da dark."

Mason snickered. "I'm sure." He lifted the young man's chin with his fingertips. "What's your name, boy?"

"Chuck," he muttered, peeking through squinted eyes.

"What the hell were you doing? You could've killed one of us. Or was that the plan?"

"No, sir," the lad mumbled. "I was told to just shoot out the windows."

Mason pressed closer. "Who told you to do this?"

"I don't know his name," he stated. "My wagon broke down just up the road and two men stopped and said they'd pay to get it fixed if I'd shoot out the two front windows in this house. They said it was just a joke. I didn't mean to hurt nobody. I'm sorry mister."

"Who were these men?" Mason probed.

The lad shook his head. "Never seen them before. The one that gave me the money rode a big pinto horse. Brown and white, I think. It was getting dark so I'm not sure."

"What did he look like?"

"Tall. Wore a buckskin jacket with fringe on the sleeves. The other had a long beard streaked with grey. He was skinny and rode a bay with a narrow blaze."

"And they didn't say why they wanted you to do this other than as a joke?"

"No, sir, that's all they said. The man on the pinto gave me five silver coins, then they rode away. They were pretty scary looking, so I did what they said."

"Hand me the gun, Pack," Mason said, without losing eye contact with the young man.

Pack placed the pistol in his friend's open palm.

Jenny rushed up and grasped Mason arm. "You're going to take him to jail, aren't you?"

He opened the chamber on the gun and dropped the three remaining bullets into his palm, then tucked them into his pant pocket. "I think he's learned his lesson, but I still intend to find out why they wanted to frighten you. There has to be more to this than a joke."

"No," she shouted. "I want him arrested. He could've killed

us."

"Just settle down," he said, removing her grip on his arm. "I'll take care of things."

"Unbelievable," she hissed. On a huff she swung around and hustled up the staircase.

His stare deepened into the lads eyes. "Now, hand over the five dollars they paid you so Miss Jones can have the broken windows replaced."

Pack released the back of the young man's shirt and the lad shoved his hand into his denim pocket and drew out the five silver coins. "I'm sorry, mister; I'll never do anything like this again. I promise."

Mason handed the lad his pistol, then glanced at Pack. "Take him to his wagon and see if you can help fix it. Use whatever tools you need from my shop or the stable. Let's get him off the road before he gets into any more trouble."

With a nod, the boy turned and followed Pack out, slamming the door behind them. Glancing down at his shirt, he assessed the damage to his chest and arm. Multiple blood splatters across the plaid cloth identified the wounds and his jaw clamped tight. Like bee stings, each lesion begged for attention. Carefully, he unbuttoned the shirt and removed the piece. Tiny fragments of glass were imbedded in his chest and across his waist line. "Ouch," he mumbled as he tried to brush the pieces away. Unable to do so, he plucked the slivers that remained intact. Once finished, he unwrapped the handkerchief tied across his injured fingers. The crimson streaks had spread and blood oozed from the wound as he unraveled the bandage. "Dammit," he grumbled. *I need to wash this and wrap it with a clean cloth.* He glanced toward the kitchen, then headed for the washroom on the enclosed porch at the back of the house. Surely there was a washbowl there. At least there was when he lived in the house.

Twenty minutes later, he dried his hands and tossed the towel onto the nearby folding table. A noise from within the kitchen caught his attention. Concern tightened his muscles and he stepped forward and shoved open the swinging door. A gasp touched his ears and he swung to his right.

Jenny, dressed in a pink robe and slippers, sunk back against the counter and grabbed her chest. "My goodness, you scared me," she said, panting. "I thought you'd gone home."

"No, I had to clean these cuts and scrapes," he said, waving his hand in front of his bare chest. "I left my shirt in the washroom. I'll leave it there until tomorrow when I go home."

"Tomorrow?"

"Yes. Thought I'd sleep on the sofa in the parlor tonight. That is if you don't mind. Don't want to leave you alone with the windows knocked out."

"Do you think they'll be back," she asked, pushing away from the sink.

"Probably not, but I'd feel better being here, just in case."

She opened the cabinet and reached for a cup, then turned back to face him. "I'm going to have a cup of coffee. Would you care for some?"

"Sure," he said, creasing a smile.

"I can't go to sleep. In fact, I may not sleep at all tonight. It's been a horrible day. I can't believe grandfather is dead. He's always been there for me." Tears welled in her eyes. "My world has completely turned upside down."

"I understand," he said, studying her every move as she placed the cups on the counter, then put the pot on the stove. "That happened to me when my mother passed. It's a terrible feeling to be all alone with no one to turn to."

She glanced once more at his bare chest. "Would you like me to get one of grandfather's shirts for you to wear? The parlor will be quite cool without the windows to keep out the chill."

"Yes, I'd like that," he replied, sliding onto the stool by the sink. She left the room momentarily, then returned with a white cotton shirt. "Here, put this on," she said. "It's going to be a little full around the waist, but at least you'll be more comfortable."

He shoved his long arms into the sleeves and began buttoning the front. When he'd finished, he grasped the shirt just above the waist and drew it tight. "I think you're right," he chuckled. "It is a bit big around the waist."

Steam escaped from the pot and she stepped over and plucked the kettle from the fire. Silence rested between them as she finished preparing the coffee, then she turned and handed him the delicate cup. "I'm still upset with you for allowing that young man to leave without punishment."

His lips touched the rim and he blew away the rising vapor, then took a sip. The warm liquid satisfied his taste buds and he stared directly into her blue eyes. He ignored the sting of her glare and his strength of control was fortified. She would not back him down, nor would she ever regulate him as she had her grandfather and stablemen. Being in charge of everything was a fantasy in her own mind...not his. She could only control those who allowed it. He restrained a snicker. This young lady had much to learn about the real world.

A bang on the back door scrambled his thoughts and his eyes narrowed.

"Someone's here," he said, his words barely above a whisper. Rising from the stool, he stepped to her side. "Get behind me," he ordered, grabbing her hand, guiding her to safety. "Don't move."

Footfalls on the back porch drew nearer. Then the doorknob rattled and the panel creaked open.

# Chapter Eight

There was a shuffling of feet, then an elderly man pushed open the door. He lowered his carpet bag to the floor and turned to help the small framed woman behind him. She brushed past and a broad smile widened her lips. "I declare, you must be Mason," she chirped. "Jenny said you were a big handsome fella."

His cheeks flushed and his tension withered.

Jenny stepped around him and spread her arms to give the woman a hug. "Agnes," she said, "I wasn't expecting you back so soon."

"Oh, shucks, we seen all that child we need to see for now," she giggled beneath her breath. "I'm getting too old to deal with babies. They're precious, but I just can't stand all the crying. Get on my nerves."

Jenny turned to Mason. "This is my maid and her wonderful husband, Walter. He takes care of the heavy chores. They've been visiting their daughter in West Virginia."

"Nice to meet you," he said, then glanced at Jenny. "I'll go now that you have someone to stay with you."

She nodded. "Thank you,' she said and exited.

\* \* \*

The next morning he locked the door to his office and started for his workshop when he spotted Jenny leaving the stable. His first instinct was to check on her. Losing her grandfather was hard enough, but the attack on her home was more than she deserved on such a difficult day. He pulled a deep breath and crossed the gravel lane to join her. "Jenny," he called as she stepped into the buggy and gathered the leather straps.

She glanced over her shoulder as he approached and lowered the reins.

Stopping at her side, he looked into her sun-washed face. "You doing all right?"

"As good as can be expected," she replied. "I didn't get much sleep. It was after ten before I went to bed. I explained everything to Agnes and Walter. They were shocked to hear of grandfather's death and said they would help me with preparations for the funeral."

"Is there anything I can do?"

"No, but I must be on my way. I must get into Lexington and get everything done so I can be home before dark. I don't like traveling on the road alone at night."

He stuffed his hand into his pocket. "Before you leave, I want to give you this," he said, pulling the five silver coins from his denims. "After you went upstairs last night, I asked the young gunman to hand over the money he got for shooting out the windows. This should cover the cost for new glass to replace them."

She hesitated, then he opened her palm and lowered the silver dollars into her gloved hand. "Take them. He should pay for the damage."

Her gaze lifted to his. "Thank you."

Seaming his lips tight, he nodded. The weight of her responsibilities left a heavy mark on her features and he felt compelled to respond. "Why don't you let me drive you into town? I need a couple of things from the general store. I can get those while you run your errands; that way, if it gets dark before you finish, I'll be there to help you get home safely."

She paused, tightened the ribbon on her bonnet, then said, "I would appreciate that. I'm not usually afraid, but with all that happened yesterday, my nerves are shot."

He smiled, then held out his hand and she lowered the reins into his open palm.

Jenny's gaze wandered along the rolling hill and surveyed the withering corn stalks in the nearby fields. "Looks like it'll soon be harvest time," she stated.

"Yes, probably another week or so the farmers will clear their land, then the crows will arrive and glean the fields. The deer also enjoy this time of year and fatten up for the long, cold winter ahead."

"It'll be different spending winter in this part of the country. I'm used to the harsh cold winters in the northeast. Also, I'll miss the lobster and bounty of fish from the sea. I always loved standing on the seashore, wearing a heavy sweater and listening to the cry of the gulls as they dove into the icy waters." She turned to him and asked, "Do you enjoy living in this part of the country?"

"I suppose. Never really thought about it. I've lived here all my life." He glanced across his shoulder. "Why, don't you think you'll like living here?"

"Oh, it's not that. Guess I'm just feeling a little homesick today."

Mason nodded to a passing rider, then turned back to meet her gaze. "Perhaps you have a beau you've left and you feeling a bit sentimental."

"No," she laughed. "I've been on a date or two, but nothing serious. In fact, I've only been kissed once, by a boy I went to school with. He took me to a church social and we walked down to the footbridge to feed the fish and he kissed me."

He chuckled. "Sounds like he didn't do a very good job."

She lowered her gaze. "No. It was awkward. He said he liked me, but when he kissed me, it was like kissing my horse."

"That bad?" he said, widening his smile.

"Well, it wasn't what I expected a kiss to be."

"No passion?"

"Nothing...maybe I just didn't like him that much." She pulled off her gloves and pushed back an annoying wisp of hair that kept fluttering across her brow. "What about you? Most your age would be married with a couple of young'uns."

He frowned "Goodness, how old do you think I am?"

"I-I mean you're nice looking." Her cheeks flushed. "I'm just surprised some girl hasn't snatched you up."

He tightened his grip on the reins as they passed an approaching carriage.

"I've never been married. Had a girl I was crazy about, but she ended up going off to school and marrying someone else."

"So she broke your heart?"

"Sure. I miss her. We had some good times together. I wonder if she's happy. Anyway, that was a few years ago. I try not to think about it because it still hurts. Maybe someday I'll find someone to fill that void in my life." He drew a breath, then clucked the horse into a trot. "Let's get to moving. This animal of yours is as slow as an old mule."

She glanced away, suppressing a giggle.

An hour later, they turned onto the main street in Lexington.

"Where would you like to go first?" he asked.

She glanced around, then spotted the shop that appeared on the top of her list. "There," she said, pointing a finger. "Drop me off at the next corner. I'll meet you back there in an hour."

He nodded and followed her direction. Once she'd stepped from the carriage, he continued on to the general store on the next street over. Sunlight glared off a metal sign, nearly blinding him as he guided the mare up to the hitching post, then shuffled up the steps and joined the bustling shoppers in the store.

"Mornin', Dan," he said, removing his driving gloves. "How's it going today?"

"Busy," he replied, drying his hand on the tail of his apron. "What can I do fer ya?"

"Oh, I need a few of the usual supplies. Coffee, eggs and a side of bacon to start with."

"You need a couple hens and a pig or two out there at your place," he laughed. "It'd save you a trip into town each week."

"You're probably right. I just don't have the place for them. 'Sides, if I didn't come in after those, I'd miss aggravating you all the time."

"Well, let me cut the material for Mrs. Madison and I'll be right with you. She's standing there with her arms crossed, patting her foot." He raised his hand beside his mouth. "You know how impatient the old women are," he whispered. "Gotta keep 'em happy."

Mason chuckled and turned away. Drawn to movement outside the window, he narrowed his eyes. A tall, slender man closed the door on the land office and shuffled down the stairs. Two strides later, he untied a large brown and white pinto from the hitching post and swung aboard. Mason's breath caught in his throat. *That looks like the man described by the young man last night.* He rushed over and grabbed the shopkeeper by the arm.

"Dan," he said, pulling the clerk away from his customer. "See that man on the pinto?"

"Yah," he grunted, frowning. "What about him?"

"You ever saw him before?"

He leaned forward. "Yes, he was in here yesterday asking for directions. Didn't buy anything though."

"Who is he?"

"Hell, I don't know. Just a stranger for all I know," he said, as the rider rode off. He turned back to his customer. "Sorry, Mrs. Madison, now how many yards did you say?"

Mason's jaw tightened. That has to be the man the boy was speaking of. Although he didn't have on a leather jacket with fringe, but why would he on a hot day like this. He glanced at the window once more, then long strides carried him out front. He held his hand above his brow and focused on the traffic moving north. The horse and rider were no longer in sight. "Damn," he growled beneath his breath. *"What's that son-of-a-bitch up to? He doesn't look like a moonshiner. Too polished. Shiners are a rough looking bunch of ruthless characters.* His gaze shot across the thoroughfare to the surveyor's office. *Hmm, wonder what he* was *doing there?* He glanced in both directions. As soon as the street cleared he darted over to the other sidewalk then entered the small office. Only one person in front of the worker remained in the room. His nerves tightened as he waited for the gentleman ahead of him to finish his business. Finally, the man turned, gave him a nod, then disappeared out the door.

Mason's palms moistened as he edged forward.

"What can I do for you, sir?" the clerk asked.

"A few minutes ago, there was a tall, slim man in here. I saw him leave and wondered if you could tell me his name?"

The man reared back in his chair and met Mason's stare with a sharp glare. "You know I can't give out that kind of information. All of our clients are treated with respect for their privacy."

"Has he been your client very long?"

"Young man," the heavy set clerk's voice deepened.

"I know," Mason broke into his words. "but someone shot the windows out of a house last night and he fits the description of the man who order the attack."

The man picked up a smoldering cigar from the nearby ashtray and stuck it in the corner of his mouth. "Then I suggest you tell the sheriff. I only survey properties. I don't watch over them."

Mason swung around and heavy steps carried him out of the building and back to the general store.

"Where'd you go?" Dan questioned. "I've got your stuff ready for you."

"Aww, I went over to the land office to see if I could find out about that guy I showed you. They wouldn't tell me anything."

"Wish I could help, but I never saw him before yesterday. " Dan greeted a lady as she came through the front door, then turned back to Mason. "He bought a twist of tobacco and a few strips of jerky. Hardly said anything the whole time he was here."

"That's all right," Mason said, lowering his chin. "I'll catch up with him sooner or later. That is if he stays in town. He may be just a drifter. Who knows?" He dropped two silver coins on the counter, then picked up his supplies and headed for the carriage. "See ya later," he called over his shoulder as he slammed the door behind him.

# Chapter Nine

*Three hours later:*

Clouds gathered overhead and a warm breeze from the north touched Mason's cheeks. He squinted and watched the 4:20 train arrive from Louisville. Discomfort gnawed at his side and he adjusted in the carriage seat, then focused on the passengers as they disembarked. Like a colony of ants, they migrated toward the luggage cart, grabbed their baggage, then hustled off the planform. Well-dressed gentlemen with their ladies at their side and traveling salesmen all scattered in different directions. He smiled. It'd been a long time since he'd travel anywhere by train. The trip that stuck in his mind was the one to New York as a child. Everything there seemed unusual. The tall buildings, streetcars, and the bicycles he clearly recalled. But, he disliked the constant noise and could not wait to get back home.

His thoughts vanished the moment Jenny appeared in the doorway. She looked so petite and fragile. The corner of his mouth lifted. Boy, he knew better than that. She was dynamite in a compact package. As she stepped from the telegraph office, a gust of wind fluttered her taffeta dress tail and she lowered her hand.

A glimpse of her petticoat widened his smile. *Too bad the wind wasn't a bit stronger.* He tied off the reins, then hustled to her side. Grasping her arm, he helped her into the buggy.

"All finished?" he asked, climbing back aboard.

She straightened her bonnet, then adjusted her position and gave a nod. "I believe that takes care of everything."

He gathered the reins. "Ready to go home?"

"Yes. I hope Agnes has dinner on. I'm famished."

"We can stop at the café near the edge of town and grab a bowl of soup to hold you over. We're still over an hour away from home, you know."

"No, I'll be fine. I wouldn't want dinner if I eat now," she replied.

He clucked the horse forward and they joined those leaving the station.

Once on the main road home, Mason eased back in his seat and glanced at Jenny. "I haven't had a chance to tell you, I believe I saw the man who paid to have your windows shot out. He was in the surveyor's office."

"Really. That's interesting. Wonder what he was doing there?"

"Don't know. I went in and asked the clerk, but he refused tell me anything."

"Are you sure it was the same man?"

He shook his head. "Not positive, but he and the horse fit the description." He glanced into her stare. "The thing that bothered me was that there was no bearded man with him. He left alone."

"So you can't say for sure, then?"

"No, but I just had a feeling this was the one the boy described."

Jenny closed her eyes and silence settled in between them.

After several minutes, he glanced over and noticed a tear rolling down her cheek. "Thinking about your grandfather?" he asked.

Her eyes fluttered open and she brushed away the moisture from her cheek. "Yes," she stated, her voice quivering. "I can't believe he's gone. And what's worse is why? Why was he shot? It makes no sense. He never hurt a soul in his life."

Mason reached over and squeezed her hand. "Don't worry. The truth will come out. Right now, everything is a mystery. I wish I had an answer."

"I hardly slept at all last night, even with Agnes and Walter being there. I know they mean well, but they are not much in the way of defense for killers or burglars. Poor Walter's eyesight is so bad he can hardly see where he is going, let alone defend us."

"Did they tell you when you ordered the new windows how long it would be before they would put them in?"

She ran her finger beneath the ribbon on her bonnet, releasing the pressure on her neck. "The man said a week to ten days."

"Would you feel better if I came over and spent the night? I could sleep in the parlor on the fainting couch as I had intended to do last night. I'd be happy to stay until the windows are installed."

"I hate to ask that of you, but I would certainly feel more at ease with you there."

He smiled. "No problem." He tapped the horse's rump with the buggy whit and the rig took a jerk as the animal responded. "I have a few chores to do when we get back, but I'll try to come over around seven-thirty or so if that will do?"

"Perfect," she said, touching his wrist. "And I'll have Agnes put on an extra plate for dinner. When I left, she said she had chicken in the oven. Please join us."

"Sounds better than left over bean soup," he chuckled.

"Good. I'll tell her to hold dinner until you get there."

He nodded and gave her a glancing smile.

Seven-thirty that evening, Mason twisted the doorbell and it gave a familiar chatter. One he'd heard so many times before, but this time he was on the opposite side of the door. An instant later, heavy footsteps arrived and the door swung open.

"Hi, Walter," he said, removing his hat and stepping into the foyer. The man lowered his chin and moved to the side.

Jenny appeared around the corner, wearing a light blue taffeta dress.

Mason's brows raised in surprise. He'd expected to see her in mourning attire.

She glanced down, then her glaze met his. "You expected to see me all in black, didn't you? Perhaps even a veil."

"Well yes

"It's all right. I understand," she said, as he hung his Stetson on the hall-tree. Then, with a smile, she grasped his wrist and led him into the dining room. "I decided not to wear black. Death is hard enough to deal with. Black only heightens the grief, in my opinion. Besides, I run a business and there's no place for grief when you're working with the public, especially in my line of work. Horse Shows are supposed to be full of life and enjoyment."

"You have a point," he said as Walter pulled the chair away from the table.

"I had grandfather's body removed and taken to the church. There's no need for a showing so we chose to send him over today. The wake will be at ten in the morning, then Walter will take him to the train station to be shipped home."

"You seem to have everything well planned," he stated as he waited for her to be seated.

"I like to keep things on a steady pace, that way I know exactly what to expect."

"I must say, you do run a tight ship," he said, slipping into his chair and dropping the linen napkin across his lap.

"Of course, that's the way it should be."

Agnes popped through the swinging door from the kitchen and placed a large wicker basket full of dinner rolls on the table, then scurried back into the kitchen. Moments later, she return with a large salad.

"Mmm," he uttered, "that looks wonderful. Been a long time since I had a green salad... and look at the size of those tomatoes? Wow."

"Walter loves to dabble in the garden. Those are all

homegrown."

Agnes retrieved two crystal bowls from the china cabinet and dished out a serving in each, then placed them beside their plates. "As soon as you finish, I'll bring out the main course," she stated with a nod. She brushed her palms across the front of her apron, then disappeared once more through the swinging door.

"She's a cheerful soul," he said, picking up his fork.

"Yes, she's a real sweetheart. She has a real good sense of humor, too."

"Good. I like that."

When they had finished dinner, the two walked into the parlor and Mason settled into the overstuff leather chair in front of the fireplace. "This seems so familiar," he said. "Just like it was before."

"I'm sure just being in this house brings back so many memories." She strode over to the mantle and plucked something from atop the piece, then turned to face him. "When Walter removed grandfather's shirt, this dropped onto the floor." She moved closer and held out her hand.

Mason leaned forward and glared at the rusty key in her open palm. He glanced up at her and pointed at the unusual metal piece. "May I?"

She nodded.

He grasped the piece, then held it up to the light. "I've never seen a key like this before. It's not a house key or for a padlock we use on the stable doors. Do you have any idea where he got it?"

"No, I've never seen it before."

He studied the piece for a moment, then said. "There are a lot of keys, but I'm thinking this may be a military key of some sort. Perhaps it was used for storing important papers or even money." His gaze lifted to hers. "Was your grandfather working for the government or serving as an officer during the war? He may have been carrying it as a souvenir in memory of a special occasion."

"I'm sure he would've mentioned it if that were so."

"I guess," he said, handing it back to her. "It certainly is an unusual piece."

"There's something else," she said, shoving her hand into the pocket of her dress. A moment later she pulled out a blood- stained cloth. "The key was wrapped in this." She unfolded the tattered piece of material and handed it to him. Much of the writing had faded and the few visible marks that remained were either covered with bloodstains or barely visible.

Mason walked over and held it close to the light. "Hmm," he uttered. "I vaguely see something here," he said, pointing near the lower edge of the cloth. "I believe it's an X. There is a faint image of a line or trail up to the mark."

"So what do you think it is?

"Not sure. Could be just a drawing or it could be a map."

She eased up beside him and glared at the piece. "You're right. It does look like a map." Her eyes met his. "A map of what?"

"That's the big question," he said with a snicker. "Could be anywhere."

She strode over and lowered into the armed chair. "Wonder

where he got it and why was the key wrapped inside? Grandfather never had any secrets. He always told me everything he was doing and why. I can't believe this is of any importance," she said, shaking her head. "He would've surely told me."

"I don't know about that. To me, there is something strange going on here. Not sure what, but I'd bet there is something far deeper than you would imagine." He started toward the leather chair beside her, then took an abrupt turn and faced the front door. "Did you hear that?"

She straightened, then glanced up. "No.'

"I could swear I heard someone yell," he said, striding toward the front door. He unlocked the bolt and gave the doorknob a quick jerk. With squinted eyes, he skimmed the shadows of the moonlit countryside, but saw nothing. As he was about to go back inside, he heard the shrill nicker of a horse. A frown creased his brow and he focused once more on the silvery moon-glow outlining the hillside.

Jenny stepped to his side. "Is something wrong?"

A moment later, the sound of an approaching horse echoed in his ears.

"Someone's coming," he said, grasping her shoulder. "Go inside and get the gun."

She nodded, then scurried away.

# Chapter Ten

Mason pressed his palm against the Corinthian pillar and strained to catch a glimpse of the oncoming rider.

The animal nickered and galloped into view.

His breath caught as he realized the horse carried no rider. It was Patruska, Jenny's beautiful young mare. Sucking a gulp of air, he surged down the steps and across the stone-walk toward the charging animal. "Whoa," he yelled, waving his arms.

The Arabian darted to the side and continued ahead at breakneck speed.

"Damn it," he muttered, then glanced at the front entrance.

Jenny shoved open the door carrying her grandfather's rifle across her arm.

"Get a wrap," he yelled. "I need your help. One of your horses is loose."

"Oh, no," she shrieked, then lowered the gun and shoved it across the nearby wicker chair. Pivoting on one foot, she rushed back into the house.

Following close behind, he entered the foyer and grabbed his leather jacket from the hall tree.

"Hurry," he said holding the door wide.

She brushed past him and ran down the steps. "Which way?' she shrieked, glancing up at him.

"Around back. Let's hope she stops soon. Don't want her getting off the property."

A dozen strides later, he grabbed her arm. "Wait," he yelled. "I have a better idea. You stay here and see if she doubles back while I get Midnight. I need to be able to catch up with her. We can't do this on foot."

"Bring Ibn, I want to go, too."

"All right. I'll be back in a few minutes."

"Please, hurry," she begged grasping his arm.

He nodded and then took off running.

The muscles in his legs burned and he fought for breath as he arrived at the barn. He doubled over to regain his strength, then focused on the stable doors. Apparently someone had broken the lock and pushed them aside. Straightening, he caught a glimpse of a horse roaming inside the stable. He gulped a breath and rushed into the corridor and turned on a light. Amber streaks of light swept across the walls of the barn as he scanned the interior. "What the hell's going on here?" All the stalls were open and only one horse remained in his enclosure. The lone animal continued to munch on the hay dangling from the feeding rack.

Mason slammed the stall gate shut and secured the lock, then swung back around. "Now where're the others?"

He peered into Midnight's stall. "Even he's gone," he mumbled, then rushed to the entrance. Poking his head around the corner, he gave a shrill whistle. Anxiety ate at him as he narrowed his eyes and skimmed the moonlit hillside. An instant later, he gave another call to his horse. Seconds passed, then he heard hoof beats. The black stallion appeared from the darkness and stopped in front of him. "Good boy," he said, taking hold of the horse's mane. With a strong grip on the thick mane, he led the beast inside.

He saddled the animal, then plucked a halter and rope from a nearby peg. Once ready, he mounted and rode out. In the darkness he spotted a small lamp shining from his friend's bedroom window. Pack always left it burning when he was gone. Just as he thought, Pack had gone to spend the night with his lady friend, Rose.

On a smile, he reined Midnight around and headed back to join Jenny.

Five minutes later, he arrived at her side.

"Where's Ibn?" she asked, grasping Midnight's bridle.

"The horses are all gone except two. Someone broke in and released them."

"Gone," she echoed in disbelief. "That's impossible. That lock's very secure."

"It doesn't keep them from using an axe on the wood around it. I believe they were willing to do whatever was necessary to get that door open.'

"How can we catch them? It's dark and they could be anywhere by now?'

He adjusted in the saddle. "You go back to the house. I'll ride out and take a look around. Maybe I can run across one or two. Lock the doors and keep the lights all on until I get back. I'll try not to be gone long. Keep that gun handy just in case those thieves come looking for something else."

She released the bridle, and then drew her wrap tight across her shoulders. "You should've brought a horse for me. I need to be out there looking, too."

"We'll both search for them in the morning. Not much chance of finding them now."

She lowered her chin and walked away.

An hour later, Mason returned to the house. Jenny opened the door for him and stepped aside as he passed and hung his jacket on the hall tree. "Well," she said, flipping the lock closed, "Did you find anything?"

"No. I thought I heard one in the thicket, but after a closer look it must've been a deer or some other critter. Even with the bright moonlight, I didn't see any of the horses."

She began crying as she walked past. "I-I don't understand. Everything has suddenly fallen to pieces. First grandfather gets murdered, then someone shoots at our house and now my beautiful horses are gone." She swung around and looked up at him. Tears rolled down her cheeks. "What's going on?" Her face washed white as flour and she leaned forward signaling she was about to faint.

He grabbed her shoulders, then wrapped his arms around her and pulled her into his embrace. "It's going to be all right. I promise." His lips brushed her forehead. "You have to stay strong. Tomorrow we'll find the horses."

"But the Wake is tomorrow. I can't be both places."

"We can tell the preacher to hold up the service. It's not like you're expecting a large crowd," he said.

She nestled her head beneath his chin. "My world has suddenly crumbled. I don't know what to do," she sobbed.

Her scent filled his nostrils and he closed his eyes to enhance the aroma. "Try not to worry," he whispered. "We'll figure this out together." He opened his eyes and took in the beauty of her flawless complexion. Her features were as perfect as a China doll. His heart beat pounded beneath his ribs and desire rushed through his veins. Taking a deep breath, he fought for composure, then whispered, "You need to get to bed so we can start early in the morning."

She nodded, then glanced up at him. "You will stay here tonight, won't you? I don't think I could sleep unprotected."

"I'll be here," he said. "You just get some rest."

He released his embrace and she stepped to the hall table and picked up the key and bloodstained map. "What shall I do with these?"

"Lock them in your safe. They may be nothing or they may be the piece that unlocks this puzzle. Nevertheless, keep it until we can find out."

He watched as she went into the study. Thoughts of her body next to his lingered in his mind. She was so small, yet so strong. The past twenty-four hours had exposed her true self. Beneath all that tough talk, she finally revealed her true nature.

Alone in her bedroom, Jenny turned on the lamp and sauntered to her dressing table. Fumbling with her dress buttons, she glanced into the mirror. "I'm a fright," she muttered, wiping a tear from her cheek. "What in God's name is happening?" She finished unbuttoning her dress and stepped out of the garment and tossed it atop the dressing screen. With shaking hands, she removed her corset and pantaloons, then slipped into her nightgown. On a jittery sigh, she removed her hair pins, then picked up the hairbrush and moved to the window. She gazed up into the heavens.

"Oh, dear God, take care of grandfather. He did not deserve to die. He was my rock...my confidant. The only person in this world I truly cared about. What'll I do without him?" Tears once again washed her cheeks. The field of stars flickered through her sorrow. "I feel so lost and alone. Please send someone to help me through this nightmare."

She stepped away from the window and tossed the brush back on the dresser, then fell across the bed. Burying her face in the pillow, she muffled her sadness.

Minutes drug by with the weight of her world in tow. Hours passed, but sleep never came. She stared into the darkness as her mind danced from one thought to another, never resolving any of the troubles taunting her. Capturing a shaky breath, she rubbed her swollen eyes and focused on the shadow of the fading moonlight that spilled across the room. Then the sound of footsteps in the hallway caught her attention. A tap on the door brought her forward. Tossing aside the satin sheet, she slipped into her robe and tip-toed to the door. "Yes, who's there?"

"Mason. It's five o'clock. I think we should head for the stable. "

"I'll be right down," she said. "Is Agnes up?"

"Yes, I asked her to fix the coffee. It should be ready by the time you are dressed."

"Give me a couple of minutes and I'll be there."

She shifted and crossed the wool rug and turned on the lamp. One glance in the dresser mirror and she moaned. "Ugh. What a terrible sight"…*and I feel as bad as I look.* She plucked the hairbrush from the dressing table and shoved the bristles into her tangled hair. Several forceful strokes and she twisted the long strands up into a knot and pinned the bun just above the back of her neck. "There, that will have to do," she said. With her mind still reeling, she grabbed her riding clothes from the wardrobe and finished dressing."

Sunlight appeared just above the hilltop as the two rode onto the main road. A flock of blackbirds lifted from the branches of the nearby walnut tree and scattered into the morning mist.

Cool air filled Mason's lungs, refreshing his thoughts from a restless night's sleep. His body ached from his wounds, as well as the unfamiliar bedding on the couch. He locked the reins around the saddle horn and snapped the buttons on his jacket. One glance at his companion and he realized she, too, was feeling the nip of the brisk morning air. "I believe fall is coming a little early this year," he said, picking up the reins. "Probably have an extra cold winter."

She nodded as Mason reined Midnight to a stop. "Which way you want to go?"

After a quick glance in both directions she pointed east. "Let's try that way."

"Good choice," he said nudging his stallion forward. "I think we should look in that swampy area first. I remember Jason and father talking about our horse Infinity getting tangled in wire there once."

"Goodness, I hope nothing that bad happens to my horses there," she said, guiding her mount up alongside him.

Less than a quarter of a mile on down the road, they met a young boy on horseback and stopped to ask if he'd seen any loose horses along the way.

"Yes, sir," he said, glancing back over his shoulder. "I saw a couple of real pretty horses grazing along the outside the Perkin's fence 'bout a half mile down the road. If I'd had a rope, I'd probably took one home with me. They sure were pretty."

"Was one of them white," Jenny asked.

"No, ma'am. They were both brown. But they sure were pretty."

Thank you, young man," Mason said. "Sounds like the ones we're looking for."

The boy nodded, then urged his horse forward.

Mason gathered the rope in his left hand, then turned to Jenny. "Well, that's a start. Let's get those animals home so we can round up the rest of them."

He slapped the rope against Midnight's rump and Jenny followed his lead.

There was much to do this day and not a minute to waste.

# Chapter Eleven

Mason pulled his pocket watch from his denims and checked the time. Just as he suspected, the hands on his father's timepiece verified noon had passed. He stepped to the window and focused on the stable. Jenny's carriage had not returned. Drawing a deep breath, he pushed the watch back into his pocket and returned to the workbench. His brows shoved together. The least he could've done was attend the funeral service. No doubt she could've used his support. Instead, he chose to continue to search for her horses.

He shook his head. Those animals were not as important as comforting her in time of such sorrow.

The annoying banging in his chest intensified. Why the hell did it matter? She wasn't his problem. He needed to concentrate on the upcoming job in Atlanta. On a huff, he grabbed a sheet of sandpaper and began working once more on the walnut desk. He'd promised a customer the piece by the weekend and he damned well better have it ready. Besides, there was much to do before he could leave for Georgia and finding Jenny's horses was not one of them. *She can deal with that when she returns.*

He sent a puff of breath against the wood and the dust scattered across his hand and onto the floor. A vision of her appeared and a grin crimped the corner of his mouth. He longed to see her smile as she had that day they first met. The thought of her blue eyes encased with long black lashes sent a tingle up his spine. Why did this please him so? She was a hellion, yet her hidden charm washed over him. Weighing less than a hundred pounds soaking wet, she was as strong-minded and bullheaded as any man he'd ever met.

He tossed the wooden piece back on the bench and threw the sandpaper into the trash barrel. *Enough, I've got to stop thinking of her.*

Heavy footfalls carried him to the front door and he stepped out onto the porch. He glanced at the stable just as Pack appeared in the doorway.

Spotting Mason, the young man raised his hand and headed toward him. "Found another horse," he yelled. "I think we have all but two now."

"Which one did you find," he asked as Pack came to a stop before him.

"The chestnut," he replied, "the one with a flaxen mane."

"Ugh," Mason groaned. "I hoped you found Ibn."

"Nope, haven't seen anything of him. I think the only other one missing is the one she calls Babe."

"Damn. Ibn is the one we need to find. That's her favorite." Mason frowned, then jammed his fingertips into his pants pockets. "I'll go back out in a bit and look some more. He's got to be out there. I want to wait until Jenny gets home from the Wake before

I go."

"She's up at her house. I passed her as I came in," Pack said with a nod. "I told her we found all but two, so she knows Ibn is still missing."

"Never thought about her not bringing the buggy back to the stable."

"Well, guess I'll saddle up and head on out then."

"Oh, before you go I have a telegram for you. The messenger brought it while you were gone this morning." He drew an envelope from his jacket pocket and handed it over.

Mason's brows lowered as he tore it open, then skimmed over the words . When he'd finished, he crumpled the paper, then glared at his friend.

"It's about the job in Atlanta. They've put it on hold. Seems there's a problem with the structure of the building. They've stopped working on it until further notice. Damn it. What else can go wrong?"

Pack removed his hat and scratched his head. "Looks like we won't be making that trip together after all?"

"Hell, no," Mason ranted, slamming the heel of his fist against the porch post. "And I've turned down two important jobs because I expected to be away for at least a month. That's just lost money."

"Sorry to hear that," Pack said, adjusting his hat back into place atop his head.

Mason stared at the distant tree line and settled his thoughts once again on the present. "Think I'll ride back and check to see if we missed one of the horses near the falls. Lot of heavy brush in that area."

"You know, I was thinkin' maybe whoever turned the horses loose may have taken those two Arabians. They were fine lookin' animals."

Mason's gaze returned to his friend. "You may be right. Don't know why I didn't think of that. Wonder if that was what they were after all along and just turned the others loose to cover their tracks."

"Sounds reasonable."

"Think I'll go back there anyway. I'd like to take a better look around where we found old man Jones. May be able to pick up a clue about why he got shot and left there. So much going on here in the last couple of days. Somewhere there has to be an answer."

"What're ya gonna do about the stills? All that needs to be carried out of the woods? I doubt they'll be back after any of it."

"I know. I'll get a couple of the stable-hands to help me in a day or so. Right now I want to see if I can find those horses."

"Do ya need me to go along with ya and help look?"

"No, you've done enough for today."

"All right, then I'm going back in my shop and start putting things away. Guess I'll start thinking about going on to Atlanta. Sure sorry you can't go. Had my heart set on our makin' the trip together."

Mason slapped his friend on the shoulder as he passed. "Good luck. I know you'll be a top student. Maybe you can teach me a few things someday," he chuckled. "Just like I taught you when we were growin' up."

"Well, ya did a good job or I wouldn't be going off to college."

Mason laughed. "One thing for sure…you'd better clean up your speech before you go or they may not keep you."

"True," Pack said, shaking his head. "But, it's so easy to fall back into my lazy way of talking."

An hour later, Mason guided Midnight beside the stream where he found Jones' body. He narrowed his eyes and skimmed the muddy shoreline. No fresh hoof-prints came into view. On a sigh, he turned and glanced upstream at the falls. The rushing water fanned out across the boulders; quiet and serene as usual. His gaze then swept across to the opposite bank. A light breeze toyed with the tangled brushwood that concealed the entrance to the cave his mother had so often warned him of. "Never go in there," she would say. "There are thousands of bats inside and they can kill you with one single bite."

He felt a chill rush up his arms.

A flock of birds suddenly lifted from the trees behind him and he turned with a jerk. The flapping wings and their cry forced every muscle in his body to wrench. "What the…" he spoke aloud as he rose in the saddle. What had frightened the birds and made them scatter? His brows tightened as he focused on the heavy underbrush. There was no movement to cause concern.

He steadied his nerves and settled back onto the leather. In all his trips to this area, none had ever bothered him until now. There was something evil in the air. A feeling of uneasiness churned in his stomach. His mouth was dry and he forced a swallow, then slid from the saddle. After securing the reins to the nearby tree, he began to inspect the grounds around the crime scene. His boot heels sunk into the terrain and the gravel crunched as he hunkered over to get a better view.

Sunlight danced in small pools of water that had formed in old tracks put down earlier. The memory came back to him as clear as a painting on the wall. He envisioned the old man's body sprawled across the branches of a fallen tree and tried to remember if he'd missed seeing anything. As he stared at the wood, a reflection beneath the limbs caught his attention. Curiosity nipped at his thoughts and he poked his finger at the metal until it popped free. He quickly gathered the coin into his palm and lifted it.

"Hmmm," he murmured, wiping the mud from the surface. Squinting one eye shut, he held it up to the light. "A Liberty silver dollar with a bullet lodged in the center," he said aloud. The corner of his mouth crimped upward. "That's strange. Never saw anything like that before."

Lowering the piece, he stuffed it into his denim pocket. "Think I'll keep that," he said.

At that moment, Midnight jerked back on the reins, nearly breaking free, and nickered a shrill whiney.

Mason swung around and glanced back into the dense underbrush. A thrashing sound emerged and he saw movement just beyond the tree line. Again, a ripple of anxiety raced up his back. Cautiously, he eased over and pulled his rifle from the sheath beneath his saddle. He cocked the trigger and worked his way toward the commotion. The muscles in the back of his neck tightened as he drew closer to the shaking thicket. His mouth dried as he lowered the rifle barrel and parted the shrub. A muted grunt came from within and he leaned closer.

Babe's head lifted then fell back with a thud and she snorted.

"Oh, no," Mason shouted, tossing the rifle to the side. He stood and stomped on the briars to flatten a path to the injured animal. "Lay still, girl," he said as he leaned closer. "I'll get you untangled. Just don't fight me."

Streaks of dried blood crossed the fallen horse's coat like the pattern on a tattered flag. Again the mare squealed in pain as she thrashed her legs to free herself from the teeth of the sharp briars. Mason locked his fingers around her halter, holding her head steady while he unwound the vicious thorns that laced her neck and muzzle. Even her mane had twisted and filled with vines and her left eye had swollen shut from the branches raking across her brow.

"Damn it, hold still," he mumbled between gritted teeth. "Ouch," he yelped as thorns tore deep into the back of his hand. He took a moment and smeared the fresh blood across the front of his jacket then quickly returned to the task at hand.

Freeing the underbrush from her head, he patted her neck and glanced down her side. Her once beautiful coat was covered with wounds. Some were visible and some were partially hidden. He pulled a deep breath and wondered if he would be able to free her from such a tangled mess.

Again, she tried to rise. At that moment, he heard the jingle of a chain. His eyes narrowed. Carefully, he moved toward the animal's midsection and scanned her rear legs wedged beneath the briar patch. Near her left hock a flash of silver-grey caught his eye. "What the heck," he muttered. "That's an animal snare." Crawling across her hip he lowered to touch the piece. The sharp edge of the wire sliced his fingertip and he jerked back. He glanced at his knuckles and saw the blood rising from the cut.

"Sonofabitch," he whined. "Somebody's been trapping this creek and Babe had to step in it." He shook his head. "Damn trappers," he said, patting her withers. "You didn't deserve that."

He rose to his feet and placed his hands on his hips. *I've got to try to get her out of here.*

On a sigh he turned and headed for Midnight to get a rope and his hunting knife he kept stored in the saddle bags. *This is going to be a far greater job than I was prepared for.*

*As* he started back to the thicket, pounding hoof-beats caught his attention and his gaze shot to the lane. A rider crested the hill. "Who the hell is that?"

# Chapter Twelve

Mason held his hand to his brow and squinted. Breaking from the shadows beneath the of birch trees, Jenny raised a hand and waved. He stepped forward and grasped the reins of the Arab's bridle as she stopped before him.

"Pack told me you came back here to look for the horses. Have you found any sign of them?" she asked leaning forward in the saddle"

That was a question he didn't want to answer. The pressure in his chest tightened. She'd suffered enough sorrow this day; she certainly did not need any bad news. He lowered his gaze and nodded. "I found Babe. She's in pretty bad shape."

Jenny grabbed the saddle horn and stood in the stirrups, then scanned the shoreline. "Where is she?"

His jaw tightened and he pointed with the handle of his hunting knife at the thicket. "In there," he said. "She's not only tangled in the briars, but has her hock caught in a snare. Won't know how bad it is until I can open the trap."

Jenny swung from the saddle and straightened in front of Mason. "What can I do to help?"

"Tie your horse over by Midnight and follow me."

She nodded and did as he said, then returned to his side.

His gaze swept from her boots to the concerning features on her face. Her casual attire was not one of a heartbroken relative. Most would be dressed all in black and wearing a heavy veil to conceal their grief. His brows lifted. "I thought you'd be in your room grieving over your grandfather."

Her mouth bowed upward. "Grandfather told me that when he died I should smile and be happy because he would be with grandmother. He said life goes on and I should make every minute that I'm on this earth count. So that's what I'm trying to do."

He tipped his head. "You're a strange young lady. Don't think I've ever know anyone quite like you before."

She laughed. "Well, I hope not. Now let's get that mare out of the stickers."

He clasped her hand and led her to the injured horse.

"Oh, my," she gasped, kneeling beside the animal.

Babe lifted her head and Jenny placed her palm on the mare's jaw and gently brushed her hand across her slick coat. "Easy, girl," she whispered and the animal lowered back on the bed of briars.

Jenny's tear-filled eyes locked with Mason's. "What can I do to help?"

"Just keep her calm while I cut away the branches across her hip and back legs. Some of these thorns are embedded. I'm sure this will hurt and I don't want her to kick me."

Jenny nodded and continued to stroke Babe's head and ears.

Carefully Mason pulled the branches apart and cut them one by one. The horse flinched, but did not fight him. Ten minutes later, he stood and glanced over the blood-splattered whelps making sure all the thorns were off. "All right," he said, "let's get her up on her feet. Not sure she can stand with the trap clapped on her hock, but I need her up to remove it."

Jenny stumbled to her feet, then gave a cluck and the horse raised on her haunches. With another tug on the lead line the mare came to a stand and lifted her hind leg. Wide-eyed, she squealed and shifted sideways. Mason pushed his frame against her withers and steadied her stance.

"Grab her halter and hold on tight while I try to open the trap," he said, easing down and placing his hand on her hoof. "Damn, that metal is really deep and her ankle is swollen twice its normal size."

"Be careful," Jenny urged. "Her ears are back. She doesn't like you messing with it."

"I know. I'm afraid she's going to jump and make it worse."

"Maybe we should get her out of here before you try to take it off. If she bolts, we all could get hung up in here."

He shook his head. "Can't," he said. "It could make things worse, then we'd have to put her down."

The frown across Jenny's forehead deepened. "No. Please… she's a good horse and she doesn't deserve to die."

"Just hang on tight and I'll try to get it off."

His fingertips had barely touched the metal when a man's

laughter rang in Mason's ears. He rose and peered over the mare's back. Two men dressed in plaid flannel shirts and denims sauntered up the creek bank chatting and laughing along the way. The bearded man carried a burlap sack while the other dangled a couple of traps over his shoulder.

"Who's there," Jenny asked her voice no more than a whisper.

"Trappers," he replied. "Hang on to Babe," he said, stepping past the horse. "Perhaps they will help us." He shoved his way through the underbrush and into the clearing. "Hey, there," he yelled. "Are you two the ones who set traps along here?"

They stopped and glanced at each other, then the bearded man stepped forward. "Yep, put them out yesterday morning. Why, you got something?"

"Sure do," Mason," said. "Got a horse with her foot caught in one of 'em."

"Oh, shit," the man hollered and ran up the bank with his companion trailing close behind. "Where?"

"Back here in the bushes… caught in a briar patch." Mason pointed a thumb over his shoulder. "Would you mind giving us a hand getting the snare off her leg?"

"Course not." The taller man said as he placed his burlap sack on a nearby rock and his partner draped the traps beside it. "Never intended to catch a horse. We're only interested in wildlife. Beaver, mink…you know, those kind of critters," the trapper puffed as he stumbled up the bank. "Hadn't considered this to be pastureland. I've not seen any horses around here before. A while back we ran into a man on horseback selling white lightening, but most of the time it's pretty quiet along here."

"This mare wouldn't have been here, except night before last someone broke into the stable and let all the horses out. We've been out rounding them up and found all but one. He's a good looking grey stallion."

"Haven't seen him but we'll keep an eye out." The man said, shaking his head. "That's a real shame somebody would do that. Any idea who it was?"

"No," Mason said as he turned and led the two up the bank.

Moments later, they joined Jenny. "This is Miss Jones," he said, gesturing toward her. "It's her horses that were released."

"Sorry about your misfortune, ma'am," the bearded man said, offering his hand. "My name is James and this here is my friend Tom."

She nodded.

"Sorry your horse got caught in one of our traps," he continued as he eased past her. "We've snared a deer before, but never a horse. In fact, we had the traps set outside the tree line hoping to catch one of the small critters that feed along the bushes." He glanced at the horse. "Guess she got excited when it snapped shut and she ran into to the bushes trying to get it off her foot."

Tom stooped down to evaluate the situation then looked up, snarling. "It looks bad. Not sure we can get it off without tearing a lot of her hide, but we'll do the best we can, ma'am."

Again, Jenny gave a nod.

James pointed at Mason. "Why don't you hold the mare's head and have the lady step back. We may be in for a fight. This mare isn't going to like it when I jerk this off."

"Good idea," Mason said, replacing Jenny's grip on the halter.

On a ragged breath, she moved aside, then stumbled from the thicket into the clearing. An instant later a commotion echoed from within and the animal squealed. Her heart pounded and her eyes widened as Mason led Babe across the trampled bushes and into view. The trappers followed close behind.

With her head lowered, the mare hobbled along and barely touched her injured foot to the ground. Blood oozed from the wound and covered the hoof.

The mere sight of the injury sickened Jenny and she swallowed back the vomit that gathered in her throat.

A loving pat on the mare's neck and Mason led the horse into the shallow water. With soothing words and a gentle motion he washed the animal's swollen hock. Soon the torn flesh appeared revealing the damage. He cringed at the sight. "Mmm, makes me hurt to look at it." He patted the animal's hip. "Stand here a moment. Let that cool water sooth it, girl," he said, then turned to Jenny. "It's going to be a rough trip back to the stable."

"Is there anything we can do? Do you think we could get the stock wagon back here to pick her up so she won't have to walk?" she asked, rubbing Babe's forehead.

"We could try, I guess," he replied, shooing a bee away from the horse's rump.

The trappers gathered their gear, then stepped near the water's edge.

"I'm so sorry," Tom said, wiping tobacco juice from the corner of his mouth. "Never expected something like this to happen."

"I understand," Mason said, then offering his hand, he continued. "Thanks for your help. I know you meant no harm."

Each man clasp his palm and turned to leave,

Mason held up a hand. "Oh, by the way, how long have you been trapping this area? I've never seen you around these parts before."

Both men swung around. "Uh, maybe a month or so. We live up river about a mile but always trapped east of here. Thought we'd try this land below the falls. Seemed like virgin territory along these banks."

"You ever seen anyone else in this area. My family has owned this land for years and rarely saw anyone. Maybe a fisherman or two," Mason said, "but recently we had some moonshiners set up shop amongst the trees back here. We finally found the place where they were hanging out and tore down their stills."

"Oh, ya," James grunted. "Like I said before, I had a fella come out of the woods and ask if I'd like to buy some fresh made white lightening." He turned to his friend. "You remember, Tom? That was the day we also saw those two riders that asked about the falls."

"What about the falls?" Jenny inquired.

"They wanted to know how far they were."

"But why?"

"Don't know. Didn't care," James replied.

Mason gave Babe a cluck and led her from the water then tied the lead rope to his saddle horn. "Do you remember anything about them?"

"Sure do. They were a weird pair. Especially the one riding that big pinto. He was dressed all in black. Looked like a preacher... and the other man was a nasty mess. Bet he hadn't had a bath in a month. Why he looked like a beggar fresh off a freight train."

"Pinto," Mason repeated, arching an eyebrow.

Jenny turned to Mason. "Didn't the lad who shot out our front windows say a man riding a pinto paid him?"

Mason nodded.

Tom spit a wad of tobacco juice on a nearby rock. "Well, they looked like trouble to me," he said, wiping his chin on the cuff of his shirt.

"Wonder what they're up too? And why would they be looking for the falls. Something strange going on here," Mason said, stacking his lips to the side as he pondered the possibilities.

"We got to be going," the bearded man announced. On a grunt, he tossed the metal traps over his shoulder and they clanged until they settled into place. He smiled, then hollered as they trekked forward. "You folks take care now. And good luck with that horse."

Mason swung aboard Midnight and tightened the lead line to the mare. An instant later, Jenny climbed aboard her mount and the two headed for the lane home. They traveled no more than ten

steps away and he stopped. "She's not going to be able to make it."
His stare met Jenny's. Why don't I stay here and you ride back and
get help? Bring the stock wagon. That's going to be the only way
we'll get her home."

Words had no more than formed on her lips when a horse
nickering cut the air. Jenny's breath caught and she swept her gaze
across the river.

The grey stallion appeared on the shoreline and reared, tossing
his head.

"Mason," she yelled. "It's Ibn.

# Chapter Thirteen

Jenny reined her horse around and bolted toward the river.

"No, wait," Mason yelled. He untied the lead rope on the mare and tossed it to the ground. On a huff, he charged after her. His heart thumped against his ribs. *Damn it, woman, stop before you drown.*

"Don't do it," he yelled.

Ignoring his plea, she made a frantic call to the stallion and he pranced along the water's edge.

A burning sensation surged through Mason and he tried to swallow back his fear. She was going into the water despite his warning. A heartbeat later, she plunged into the river and called for her beloved Ibn once more.

The stallion nickered and tested the waters along the rocky shore.

Jenny's mount began to swim but the current quickly caught him and pulled them westward.

"Hang on," Mason yelled. "I'll get ahead of you and help you out." He dug his heels into Midnight's sides urging the beast faster along shoreline. A spray of rock and sandy mud ejected from the horses hooves as he fought to gain on the fast-moving current.

"Oh, please hurry." she pleaded. "I don't know how long I can hang on," "The water is deep and we are being pulled under."

"There's a bend in the river just ahead," he shouted. "Go to the south bank, the water's calmer there. I'll grab you."

"I'll try," she said, struggling to stay on the animal's back. She jerked the reins and forced the horse to the left. The water crashed against her legs numbing them as it tossed her against the many boulders along the way. Her cries were muffled as she washed from the saddle and onto the beast's rump. She tightened her grip on the slick leather straps. The waves splashing across her face blurring her vision. On a gasp, she slid from the animal's back. A choking cough followed each breath. In desperation, she grabbed for the steed's tail. Her fingers entwined the thick hair, but soon released the long strands as her strength weakened. She could no longer fight the powerful current. Everything surrounding her grew dim. Even the sounds of the rushing current seem distant.

Mason arrived at the bend in the river and guided Midnight into the water as far as he dared. Any deeper would put his life in danger as well as his horse. Estimating her point of arrival, he maneuvered his steed into place. "Easy, big fella," he said as Midnight nervously flicked his ears.

He narrowed his eyes. Jenny's horse came in to view...but where was she?

Moments later, sunlight reflected on her limp body as it tumbled through the water like a ragdoll. His breath caught. "No," he yelped. Frantic, he dove in and swam toward her. In desperation, he fought to reach her. A barrage of splashing waves blinded his vision, yet he continued. A heartbeat later, he grabbed her arm, just as the current swept them into a small cove. Securing his grip, he guided her to shore. Relieved, he steadied his footing on the gravel shore. His hands grasped her waist, then he lifted her, drawing her into his arms.

On a sigh, he carried her up the bank and then placed her on the grassy knoll. Carefully, he rolled her on her side. With an open hand, he thumped her back. She wrenched then gagged, expelling a rush of water. Coughing, she pulled away and more liquid sprayed from her lips. Resting on her palms, she struggled to rise. Mason grasped her shoulders and helped her into a sitting position.

"Better?" he asked, steadying her small frame against his shoulder.

She nodded, then eased her eyes open.

He smiled.

"I- I'm...," she sputtered.

"Don't try to talk. Just sit there a few minutes. You're all right." He placed his arm across her shoulders and brushed dripping strands of hair from her face. "Just take it easy. Catch your breath."

She nodded once more.

He glanced downstream just in time to see her mount stumble from the river.

"You rest," he said, pushing to his feet. "I need to get the horses." He turned and gave a whistle. Nickering, Midnight cantered to him. Grabbing the reins, he swung into the saddle. A slap of the leather and they galloped away.

A few minutes later, he returned. "It'll be dark soon. If you feel up to it we should head home."

"Yes," she replied and staggered to her feet, her head still spinning from the shocking experience.

He jumped down and helped her into the saddle. "You sure you feel like riding?"

She pulled in a deep breath. "I'm sure."

With a nod, he swung aboard Midnight and started for the road home.

"Where's Ibn? Have you seen him?" she asked glancing at the other shore. "I thought he came in the river when I did."

"No," Mason replied. "When you went into the water he turned and ran back into the woods.

"Oh, my, I may never see him again," she said, whimpering.

"Can't worry about him right now. We need to get home." He declared.

She skimmed the horizon and her injured horse came in to view. "What about her?" she asked, pointing a trembling finger.

"I'm going to tie her up and come back later," he said.

"But shouldn't one of us stay with her? She may get attacked by a wild animal."

"That's a chance we'll have to take," he said, guiding his horse toward the injured animal. "I'll come back with a wagon as soon as I can. She sure can't walk that distance on a swollen foot."

Jenny sniffled. "She looks so pitiful."

"She'll look better once I get her home and clean her up. The main thing is to get medicine on that cut. Don't want it getting any worse." He pulled back on the reins. "Wait here while I take care of this," he said and rode off to catch Babe.

Within minutes he snapped the lead to her halter and secured her to the limb on a nearby pecan tree. Once the job was finished, he returned and they continued their trek home.

Darkness blanketed the hillside and Midnight set the pace, cantering toward the stable.

Overhead, wispy clouds floated past the moon and stars. Nearby, crickets joined in harmony with resident frogs chanting their love for peace and tranquility. Such perfect surroundings only masked the danger Mason and Jenny had faced in hours past. How well nature covered the imperfections of real life.

Jenny expelled a sigh of exhaustion. A warm bath and a soft bed could not come soon enough. She guided her Arab into the stable and Mason followed close behind. He, too, would have welcomed a bath and bed, but there was still much to do.

He took a deep breath and slid from the saddle. "You go on up to the house. I'll take care of your horse."

"Are you sure? I can help."

"No, I'm going to see if Pack is awake. I'll get him to go with me. You get some rest."

She handed him the reins and shuffled out the doorway.

*Poor girl, she's been through hell today.* He shook his head, then unsaddled her horse and bedded him down for the night.

Twenty minutes later, carrying a lantern, he made his way to the bungalow just beyond the workshop. A quick rap on the door and he stepped back to await a response. Moments later the door creaked open and Pack, dressed only in long johns, peeped around the edge. "What the hell do you want?" he asked, widening the opening. "Don't you know it's nearly midnight?"

"I need your help," Mason said, shoving his friend aside as he entered. "We found one of the horses and she's hurt. I need to hitch up the wagon and go after her."

"Now? Can't it wait until morning?" He perched his hands on his hips. "Damn it, Mason, I'm in no shape to go out this time of night. I just finished off my jug of white lightening. Hell, I did good to walk to the door."

"Where'd you get that?" Mason asked, glancing around the room in search of the empty container. "I thought you didn't drink?"

Pack's features tightened, "Well, I didn't. I just wanted to try it." He drew his lips sideways. "If you must know, I found it when I tore down the stills the other day." He lowered his chin and glanced away. "I couldn't resist." His gaze returned to Mason. "It was pretty good, though."

Mason deepened his glare. "Get dressed. We're wasting time. I'm tired and in no mood for excuses."

Guilt ate at the young man. Understanding his friend's need, he swung around and headed for the bedroom. "Give me a minute," he grumbled.

"Good," Mason said. "Meet you at the stable. I'll get the harness on your horse. He's good at pulling wagons."

Still grumbling, Pack raised his hand and waved him on.

An hour later the wagon rattled to a stop beside Babe. With head lowered, she barely moved as Mason jumped from the wagon. He grasped the handle on the lantern and walked to her side. "You ready to go home, old girl," he asked, rubbing his hand along her neck. The briars in her mane scraped his fingertips as he gave her a loving pat, then moved the light along her side and glanced down at her injured foot. Still swollen, blood oozed from the wound and dried in streaks across her hoof. "Mmm," he groaned. "That needs cleaned again."

Pack lumbered up beside him. "Wow," he said, removing his hat and scratching his head. "She sho is a mess."

Mason turned with a frown. "What?"

"Sorry." He offered a sheepish grin, his snow white teeth illuminated by the flickering light. "She sure is a mess."

Mason untied the rope from the tree. "Here, hold this," he said passing the lead to his friend. "I'm going down to the river. Got to wet my kerchief so I can clean that hock. Can't let that wound close dirty." He swung around. "There's a bucket of grain in the wagon. I'll bring it over. You can feed her while I'm gone."

Pack nodded then settled his hat back into place. A rustling in the thicket nearby drew his attention. He stepped past the horse and narrowed his eyes. Again the bushes moved and a branch cracked. The young man's brows lifted. "Hey, Mason," he called, lowering the tone of his voice to just above a whisper. "Come here."

Mason grabbed the bucket and hurried back to his friend's side. The light spilled over the area as he held up the lantern. "What's wrong?"

"Shh," Pack said, placing a finger across his lips, then pointing at the nearby undergrowth. "Something's in there."

Mason eased forward. His throat tightened as he held the light closer to the bush. A soft nicker touched his ears.

"What is it?" Pack asked, peering over his shoulder.

"It sounded like a horse," he said. Carefully, he separated the shrubs, then held the light higher. The animal pushed its head in front of Mason's face and he jerked back in surprise. "Ibn," he yelped. "Oh, my God, it's Jenny's horse." He grabbed the animal's halter and led him into the clearing. Rubbing his hand across the beast's withers, he said, "How about that? Never expected to find him like this."

Pack chuckled. "We got a two-for-one deal."

"What a relief. He sure looks like he survived much better than Babe. I don't see any cuts or marks on him. That's good news. Don't need any more injuries. I'll tie him to the back of the wagon after we get her loaded. Jenny's going to be so happy." He clucked the horse forward. "Let's get moving."

"Sounds all right to me," Pack said. "My head's a poundin' like a sonofabitch. In fact, I think I'm gonna puke."

Mason laughed. "That's what you get for drinking that homemade shit."

"Don't think I want anymore," he admitted. "Let's hurry. I need to get home."

# Chapter Fourteen

Jenny stood before the dressing table and stared into the mirror. She raised her hand to her shoulder and brushed her fingertips across the purple lump, then slid her hand down her arm. Everything hurt. Thumping against those boulders the day before had taken its toll. A frown creased her forehead. *What was I thinking? I should never have tried to cross that river. I just wanted my precious Ibn back. He's probably gone forever.*

She pulled the robe back across her shoulder and glanced at the clock on the chest of drawers. Eleven forty-five. On a heavy sigh, she sauntered over to the wardrobe and opened the door. She needed to go to the stable and check on Babe, but all she really wanted to do was crawl back into bed. Another sigh followed and she sealed her lips tight. *I really should stop over and thank Mason for saving my life. I can't think of a time I've been more frightened.* She shuffled through her clothes and picked out her favorite work dresses. With a slight jerk, she removed it from the hanger and draped it across the foot of the bed. A cutting pain shot up her back as she straightened. In a flash, her hand gripped her waist. "Mmm,"she moaned. She turned and flopped down on the edge of the mattress. "I'm miserable," she spouted out loud. "I'll never make it to the barn." She fell back on the bed and stared at the ceiling. Tears rolled from the corners of her eyes. *This is awful. I hurt all over.*

She dabbed her eyes with the sleeve of her robe, then sat up. *Enough. I must be strong and overcome this self-pity. There's work to do. I'll take something for the pain and be on my way.*

A knock on the door brought her around. "Who's there," she called out.

"Agnes. Are you all right, Miss Jenny? You didn't come down for breakfast and it's nearly lunch time."

Jenny stepped to the door and opened the panel. "I'm fine," she replied. "Just fix me some coffee and one of those muffins you had left over from yesterday."

"Yes, ma'am," the maid said, peeping over Jenny's shoulder. "I'll get your linens changed today and freshen up your room. Is there anything else I can do for you?"

"As a matter of fact, there is. I took a fall yesterday and I'd appreciate it if you'd fetch me some pain medicine to take with my meal."

"Yes, ma'am, I'll put it on your plate," she said with a nod.

The woman pivoted, then scurried down the hallway.

Jenny stepped back and closed the door. *There is no need for her to know what a silly thing I did.*

Again she rubbed her waist and hip, then removed her gown and robe. One glance down and she shuddered. Scrapes and bruises dotted her skin. She seamed her lips tight. Splashes of red, blue and purple reminded her of a patchwork quilt that once adorned her bed. *Thank God these will be covered by my dress.*

A quick about-face and she went to the chest of drawers and pulled out a snow white petticoat and corset, then dressed and went downstairs.

She glanced out the window as she entered the parlor. Sunlight sparkled through the new glass panes and brought a smile to her lips. It was good to have the house in order once more. A glance to the left and she took a moment to check her skirt-tail in the mirror beneath the hall table. Satisfied all was well, she continued on to the dining room. Another splash of sunlight through a nearby window welcomed her as she slid into her favorite chair at the long Cherrywood table. Fanning out the linen napkin she placed it across her lap. The aroma of fresh brewed coffee captured her attention and she lifted the china cup and took a sip. "Mmm," she uttered, closing her eyes. In her mind, there was nothing more pleasing than hot coffee to start her day. *This will be a good day. Of that I'm sure.* She would put the past to rest and expect nothing short of the best on such a lovely morning.

A half hour later, she made her way down the private path and entered the stable. Workmen busy grooming glanced up and nodded as she made her way down the corridor. Immediately, her attention swept toward the banging in Ibn's stall. Her heart skipped a beat as she rushed over and peered over the gate. The prize stallion paused and looked her way. "Ibn," she shrieked and swung open the door. Her skirt-tail gathered fragments of the sawdust bedding as she scurried to his side. Tears welled in her eyes. She hugged his neck and pressed her cheek to his. "I never thought I'd see you again," she muttered. Delighted, she ran her fingers through his long silver mane, then straighten the long strands of hair between his ears.

"So you found my surprise," Mason said, stepping up behind her.

She turned and met his smiling face. "Yes. Where did you find him?" she asked, still caressing the animal's withers.

"He was grazing near Babe when we went to pick her up. Couldn't believe it. He was easy to catch."

"He's a good boy," she said, patting the beast. "Thank you so much. And I want to thank you for saving my life yesterday. I thought I was going to die."

With a chuckle, he shook his head. "I thought so, too. I'm just glad it turned out all right."

She glanced across the corridor. "What about Babe? How is she?"

Ibn lowered his head and continued eating his feed.

"Come," Mason said, guiding her onto the walkway. "I put her in the end stall after we cleaned her up and I checked on her this morning. The swelling in her leg seems to have gone down but the wound still looks pretty nasty."

Jenny peeked between the stall slats and swept her gaze over the injured animal. "She looks so pitiful. She has to be miserable."

"It'll take a few days for it to heal, plus she has all those scrapes and cuts from the briars. But, she'll be fine."

His gaze dropped to her lips and the thunder inside his chest intensified. Full and as red as a summer rose they called to him. He could imagine covering them with his own, tasting their sweetness. Every hormone in his body raced to his groin. She was beautiful. Even with scrapes and bruises on her cheek, he fought to hide the desire that ran rapid through his veins. Choking down a swallow, he forced his gaze to the side, hoping she had not picked up on his admiration.

"Yes, yes, I'm fine. I need to get back to work. I saw you come down the lane and thought I'd catch your reaction to Ibn being back."

"I'm delighted," she said with a grin, then reached up and hugged his neck. "Thank you so much for all you have done for me. I do appreciate it. Perhaps I can do something special for you someday."

He smiled and chuckled beneath his breath. *Could be.* He headed for the doorway, but took a moment to pause and glance back at her. Perhaps she wasn't such a hellion after all. Another smile creased his lips and he stepped outside.

A breeze rippled the sleeves on his shirt and picked up the dust around his boots as he shuffled along. A shadow swept over the landscape. His gaze darted to the clouds gathering overhead. *Looks like we may have some rain on the way. I should bring Midnight in from the pasture. Don't want him caught out in a thunderstorm.*

He changed his direction, then stopped short when he heard a rider coming down the lane from the main road. He squinted. Was it a customer or a visitor?

The lone rider waved, then continued forward and stopped in front of him. Dressed in a white shirt, black leather vest and dark trousers, he stepped from the saddle. "You're just the one I want to see," he said, his voice deep and raspy.

"What brings you out here, sheriff?" Mason asked, extending his hand.

The man grasped his palm and gave it a firm shake, then glanced over his shoulder as a worker led one of the horses to the pasture. "Can we go inside? I need to speak with you in private."

Mason lowered his brow in concern. Sheriff rarely made house calls. "Follow me," he said and led the man into his office and closed the door behind him.

"Have a seat," he said, pointing at the walnut chair in front of his desk. "Must be something important to bring you all the way out here?"

"As a matter of fact, there is," he said as he eased into the chair and crossed his legs. "There are a couple of things I need to talk to you about."

Mason backed up and perched his hip on the corner of his desk. "Well, I'm glad you came out, because I've wanted to see you, as well. Just hadn't had the time. Been a lot going on around here. You go ahead and say your piece and I'll tell you mine when you're finished."

The sheriff nodded, then removed his hat and placed it on his lap. On a fresh breath, his gaze met Mason's. "I believe Brad Collins used to work for you."

"He sure did and I'm going to hire him again when my contract in Atlanta is reinstated. There are some structural issues with the building right now, but soon as they're corrected, we should begin work on that job. Why? What about Brad?"

The sheriff dropped his gaze for a moment, then met Mason's once more. "I have him in jail."

"Jail? What the hell for?"

"He killed Doc Johnson."

"What," Mason shouted, coming to his feet. "Brad? You must have the wrong person. He wouldn't do something like that. Are you sure?"

"Yes, even had a witness. Mrs. Thompson and her daughter came into the office and saw them scuffling, then Brad slammed Doc up against the brick wall. Knocked him out cold. Brad stole some medicine, she said, and ran out the door. Next day, Doc died. I arrested Brad and he's in jail now facing murder charges."

Mason shook his head. "I can't believe it. That's terrible. Brad may be a little slow on the job, but he'd never hurt anyone. So, what can I do?"

"He asked me to fetch you. Says he needs a favor." A nervous twitch tugged at the corner of the man's mouth. "I told him I would ask."

"Sure. I'll come. In fact, I'll close my shop and ride back in town with you."

"He'll appreciate that and so will I. I feel so bad about arresting him, but I had no choice."

"What else was it you need?" Mason asked, crossing his arms against his chest.

"I was over at the saloon yesterday and the bartender told me about a couple of men asking about your family's estate."

"Oh, I sold that a while back to a man and his granddaughter. They bought the stable, too. They've been living there for a while now. Actually, that's one of the reasons I wanted to see you. The old man went back by the falls one day and somebody shot him. Could've been a hunter...but I doubt it. Also, there's been a lot of strange things going on around here lately."

The sheriff put his hand up to his chin and pondered for a moment. "I don't think these men were wanting to buy the place. They were asking a lot of questions about the history of the property. Had something to do with the war back in the 60's."

"'Tween the North and South?"

"That's what I was told."

"Can't think of anything special happening around these parts. I know troops traveled these roads and back country a lot, but never knew of anything else." Mason's stare deepened. "What did these men look like?"

"Didn't get a real good description. Said the one that asked all the questions wore all black and the other was a scruffy fella with

Christine Wissner

a long beard."

Mason straightened, dropping his arms to his sides. "That sounds like the two I wanted to ask you about. It's for sure those fellas are up to no good. Do you know where they're staying?"

"At the hotel, I think."

"I need answers." Mason said, heading for the door. "Let's get going."

# Chapter Fifteen

As the two rode into Lexington, Mason glimpsed at the departing thunderheads. Sunlight broke through the clouds. What a welcome sight after riding through a heavy downpour. He grabbed the brim of his hat as a gust of wind whipped debris across the street, scattering the rubble along the thoroughfare.

A few blocks later, he reined Midnight to a stop near the jailhouse and slid from the saddle. Stiff from riding, he stretched, then removed his Stetson and brushed away the moisture. Settling it back on his head, he took off his slicker, gave it a shake, then folded the piece and stuffed it into his saddlebag.

On a quick turn, he followed the sheriff into the jail. The stale smell of cigar smoke soured the air, leaving a nasty taste in his mouth. He frowned. Suppressing a cough, he halted by the doorway and waited while the man stopped at his desk to pick up the cell keys.

The deputy sitting at a nearby table glanced up and peered over his wire rimmed glasses. "Afternoon," he grunted and gave a guarded grin.

Mason nodded.

"Anyone been in?" the sheriff asked his assistant as he pushed the drawer shut.

"Naw," the burly man replied. "Just another boring day on the job."

"Well. you could be up sweeping out front instead of reading that newspaper all the time," the sheriff snapped. "Your broad ass is going to take root in that chair if you don't get up once in a while."

The man stood and kicked the chair aside. On a huff, he grabbed the broom and rushed out the front door, grumbling beneath his breath.

Movement in the next room drew Mason's attention. He swallowed hard as he caught a glimpse of his friend. Brad shuffled his feet and rose from a cot. Yawning, he stepped over and grasped the iron bars. Mason's heart sank. That was a sight he'd never imagined.

"Mason," Brad called out. "That you?"

"Settle down," the sheriff said. "I'm bringing him." He opened the door and stepped aside to allow Mason to enter. "Ya got fifteen minutes to get your talkin' done. Not a minute more." He shot a hard stare through squinted eyes, then locked the door and left the room.

Mason swallowed back his disapproval, then turned to Brad. "Is he always that grumpy?"

"Not always," he shrugged.

"He said you sent for me and you had killed the Doc. Good Lord, man what the hell were you thinking?"

"I needed medicine for my wife and I didn't have the money to pay for it. Didn't realize it would be that expensive. Anyway, he wouldn't let me have it." His eyes teared. "Marg was sick. Real sick. I pleaded with him. Told him I'd bring it to him later, but he said no. He said he was short on that medicine and wouldn't get another shipment for two week and I could come back then. I knew she wasn't gonna make it that long without it, so I had to take it."

"Why didn't you come to me? You knew I'd let you have the money."

"I was afraid to wait," he said as a tear rolled down his cheek. "And I was right. She died that night. Now, my Marg is gone and I'm going to prison. I didn't mean to kill him...I just wanted the medicine."

"When do you go before the judge? Maybe he'll let you off easy because you were desperate and you didn't mean to kill him. After all, you've never done anything like this before." He rested his shoulder against the iron bars. "It sounds like an accident more than a murder."

"Sheriff says I'm probably looking at fifteen to twenty years."

"Still, that's a lot," Mason said, shaking his head. He stared at his friend for a moment then asked, "What about your son? Where is he?"

"Danny's staying with a neighbor. I don't have any relatives close by. Guess when I get sentenced and find out how much time I'll get, then I can decide if I'm going to send him to an orphanage.

He doesn't deserve that, but I don't know what else to do."

"I agree. He's a nice boy and that would ruin his life. He needs someone who will love and care for him."

"That's why I had the sheriff get you. I know you aren't married, but I thought you might consider keeping him for me. Danny looks up to you. He talks all the time about how you saved his kitty. You're his hero."

Mason straightened. "Well, I don't know about that. I like the boy, but I don't know anything about raising a child."

"Please, Mason, you'd give him a good home and raise him proper. I know you would."

"That's a lot to ask of a single man. Besides, I work all the time. What would I do with him while I'm working? And you know I'm out of town for weeks at a time on different jobs. They could contact me any day about the contract I have in Atlanta."

"Oh, please, Mason. I don't want to put him in an orphanage. He doesn't deserve that."

"You know I would help you if I could. I just can't."

Brad sat down with a thud on the side of the bed, then lowered his head and began to sob.

Mason stepped over and placed his hand on his friend's quivering shoulder. "I'm sorry. " Sadness tugged at his heart. But, what could he do? What could he say to comfort this grieving soul? "I'll ask around. Perhaps I can find someone who'll help. If I do, I'll let you know."

The man covered his eyes and gave a slight nod.

"Don't give up, Brad." Mason said, patting his friends back. Tears welled in his eye and his throat tightened as he called for the sheriff. The keys rattled in the man's palm as he approached and unlocked the cell door.

Mason shook his hand, then said, "If I haven't returned before the sentencing, let me know. I'd like to be here for the judgement."

"Sure thing," he replied.

With a nod, Mason stepped out the side entrance and the door clicked shut behind him. He trekked to the front walk and scanned the busy street and surrounding buildings. *What a dilemma. Poor Brad has the weight of the world on his shoulders. I feel so bad for him. And the boy. What a life- changing experience this will be for him. How terrible. God, I wish there was something I could do for them.*

He narrowed his eyes and focused up the street at the Madison Hotel. A few long strides and he gathered the reins and lifted into the saddle. A short ride later, he arrived at his destination. Several patrons were exiting the popular guesthouse and offered a smile as they brushed through the doorway. Stepping inside, Mason's gaze swept the busy lobby and was taken by the beauty of the old lodging. The walls were covered with blue and gold flocked wallpaper and the chairs were covered in royal blue velvet with tufted backing. How impressive. He skimmed the woodwork on the ceiling adorned with two large crystal chandeliers that glittered overhead. "Damn," he muttered beneath his breath. "This place is really something. "

He straightened, then strode to the registration desk and

tapped the small gold bell. A middle-aged man wearing a white shirt and embroidered vest looked up. Placing his pen on the countertop, he came to greet Mason. "Yes, sir, may I help you?" he asked.

"I'm looking for a couple of men. I understand they have been staying here. Don't know any names. Just know one is usually dress all in black and rides a big brown and white pinto. The other is a scruffy fella with a long greying beard."

"I think I know the ones you are referring to, but I can't give out names of our guest. They've been here off and on for a week or two, but they checked out this morning."

Mason leaned closer. "Did they mention where they were headed?"

"No, I didn't hear them say." He glanced over at his co-worker. "Hey, Ned, did that strange pair you checked out this morning mention where they were going?"

The clerk chuckled, then nodded and glanced back at Mason. "Sorry, they're an unusual pair. The one seems very intelligent and the other…well, let's just say he's not too smart."

"So I've heard," Mason said.

"No," the co-worker said. "But said they'd be back in a day or two. Said they had some unfinished business near here."

"Thanks," Mason said, tapping his palm against the counter top. "I'll try to catch them another time."

Disheartened, he pivoted and headed for the door. Lost time with no results. He'd go see the bartender the sheriff mentioned, but the place did not open until six. He'd have to catch him another time.

Depression set in as he swung aboard his horse and headed home.

Two hours later, he arrived at Crystal Falls. The workers had finished their job for the day and the old collie rose from her nap to greet him. He eased from the saddle, then patted her head. "You guarding the place?" he asked. "Good girl." The building seemed so quiet with everyone gone. Pigeons cooed from the rafters and Mason ducked as one flew out when he widened the door. With a tug on the reins, he led Midnight inside, removed his gear, then brushed the stallion down before putting him in the stall.

Still heavy in thought about Brad and his son, he backed up and sat on a bale of hay. What the hell could he do to help them? He didn't know how to raise a child. Being the youngest in his family, the only other children he knew were those his own age. He removed his hat and placed it on the barrel beside him. Brad would just have to get someone else for that job. He raked his fingers through his hair. There had to be someone, somewhere.

A rustling outside the door brought him around. An instant later, Jenny came into the barn. "Hi Mason," she said in a gleeful chortle. "Where is everyone?"

"Don't know. I just got here and the place was empty. Guess everyone's gone home for the day." He raised a brow. "What're you so happy about?"

"I got a letter from a man in Virginia that has a prize Arabian mare and wants to breed her to my Ibn," she giggled. "Isn't that wonderful? He said he had several people that recommended my horse. They'd seen him in a show I had Ibn in up in New York. He won Grand Champion. I still have the ribbon hanging in my room."

"That's great. I suppose they'll pay a sizable fee for stud service."

"Oh, yes. I get several hundred dollars." She wrapped her arm around the post next to her and pressed against the wood.

Mason creased a smile. "And when is this event going to take place?"

"Next week." She placed her cheek against the back of her hand. "I expect near the weekend. Usually they leave the mare for a few days to make sure the breeding is successful."

He chuckled. "I'm well aware of the process. We bred a lot of thoroughbred over the years."

"Yes," she said as she straightened. "I forget your family was in the horses business, too." She stared at him for a moment then moved closer. "You look troubled."

"As a matter of fact, I do have something on my mind."

She sat down on the bale of hay beside him. The twinkle in her eyes faded. "What's wrong?"

"One of my foremen is in jail and he has a young boy that he may have to put in an orphanage. He asked me to take the child and keep him until he gets out."

"Will he be there long?"

"Probably years. He hasn't gone before the judge yet, but I'm sure it'll be quite a while."

"Oh, my," she muttered. "Where's the mother?"

His brow lowered. "She's dead." His stare intensified as he told her the whole story. "So you see, the child will have to start a new life. It's going to be hell for him."

"So there's no one at all he can turn to?" she asked. "How old is the lad?"

"I don't know for sure. Maybe six or seven. I'm not a good judge of age. Especially in children."

She stood and paced a few steps back and forth in front of him, then turned and locked her gaze with his. "Hmmm, I may have a solution."

"You do?" He straightened up. "What… what would that be?"

"Easy, now." She held her palm up to his chest. "I'll have to ask first, but I may be able to help." She turned and headed for the door. "I'll tell you tomorrow." With a smile and a wink she ducked out the door.

# Chapter Sixteen

The following day, a rap on the door pulled Mason's attention from his work. He lowered his hammer and placed it on a nearby workbench. One glance out the window and he found Jenny patiently waiting. He smiled, then trekked to the entrance and swung open the door.

"Come on in," he said, stepping aside. "Cool this morning, isn't it?"

"Yes, I should've worn a wrap."

"I have a jacket over there," he said, pointing at the rack on the side wall. "You're welcome to use it."

"I'll be fine," she said, rubbing her upper arms. "I'm heading for the stable. I have something there I can put on. I just wanted to stop by and tell you I spoke with Agnes and her husband last night about the boy."

"Agnes. Your maid?" His brows lifted, then he pushed the door shut and faced her. "Is she the one you thought would care for him?"

"Yes. They had a son. The boy was seven years old. Ten years ago they lost him in a horrible accident. Since then, she has begged her husband for another child. He always told her no, not yet. He felt the accident was his fault."

"What happened?"

She drew a breath and steadied her stance. "Well, he was out plowing one day and the boy was playing near their grain silo. Suddenly it collapsed and it came down, catching him beneath its weight."

"How terrible," Mason said, shaking his head. "I've heard of things like that happening. "

She frowned. "He'd warned the boy not to play near it, but like most young'uns, he didn't always do as he was told."

"I understand the man feeling guilty. Children… they just don't realize the danger. I was constantly getting a spanking for doing things I shouldn't. Mother would tell me not to and I'd go right ahead anyway. It's a wonder I didn't get hurt."

She giggled beneath her breath. "Boys are just more daring than girls."

"So what did they say when you told them about Danny? Will they help?"

"They talked it over last night and told me this morning they'd love to take him. I said I'd let them have an extra room to be his and he can stay as long as he behaves. I'm sure it'll be a big adjustment for all of us, but we're willing to give it a try. I'm sure they'll treat him as their very own. My concern is will he want to go back to his father when he gets out of prison."

Mason drew his lips to the side. "Hmm. I guess we'll have to cross that bridge when we come to it. The boy may be grown by then."

"True," she said. "I'm sure it'll be difficult on all of us at first. I've never dealt with a young'un in the house before. And heaven knows, I'm not ready to be a mother figure."

He laughed. "You'd be a beautiful mother."

Her surprised look wiped the smile from his face and warmth rushed to his cheeks. "Well, you would."

"Thank you, but I'm sure that day is a long way off."

She started to turn and he grabbed her upper arm and pulled her to him. Their eyes met and he could no longer resist. His mouth covered hers. She started to push away, but instead melted into his embrace.

His heart thundered as her breasts touched his chest. He'd silently longed for this moment. Her lips encased in his as desire bubbled through his body and settled in his groin. He didn't want the warmth of her small frame to ever leave his embrace. Her lips parted and he seized the opportunity to enter, touching her moist, enticing inner soul. Passion raged for a moment then vanished as he pulled away. Their eyes met once more. "I-I shouldn't have done that," he whispered. "Sorry. You're just so beautiful, I ..."

She placed a finger across his lips. "Sssh," she said softly. "It's all right." She seamed her lips tight, then stepped back and scurried to the door. A quick glanced over her shoulder and she rushed out, pulling the door shut behind her.

Transfixed, he stared out the window, gazing at her as she

disappeared into the stable. *What the hell have I done? Surely she liked it. If not, she would've smacked my face. Women, why are they so complex? Now she knows I care. Maybe it's too soon… but I couldn't resist. What a fool I am to think she might care for me. It's just these last few days she has changed. Softer, more like the girl I've dreamed of, but never found.* He took a deep breath and released a slow sigh, then smiled. The taste of her lips lingered in his mind. One thing for sure, he certainly did enjoy it.

Two hours later, Pack gave his signature rap on the shop door, then swung it open.

"Hi, Pack, what's up?" Mason said, placing the strip of wood he just sanded on the cluttered workbench. He faced his friend and propped his hand on his hip. "I was planning on coming over to see you this evening after I finished work. Wanted to find out when you're leaving for Atlanta."

"That's why I stopped by," he said. "I'm going by to see Rose tonight, then leaving first thing in the morning. I'm packed and ready to go. I just wanted to drop off the key to my house, in case you should need to get in. As for the shop, you don't need a key to that. You can go in anytime you need something, you know that. I should be back in two or three weeks. In fact, I may be back sooner if they don't accept me," he chuckled.

"You'll do fine, my friend," he said, slapping Packs upper arm, then shook his hand. "Good luck and be careful. Gonna miss you."

"Ya, miss you too," he said as tears welled in his eyes. He bit his lip for a moment, then turned and grasped the door handle. "See ya," he said, his voice crackling. Lowering his chin, he turned and swept through the entry and the wood rattled shut behind him.

Mason stood silent for a moment, pondering about days gone by and how they'd been friends from childhood. He loved that big guy. Never had he been closer to anyone than he was to Pack. They had a bond that very few experience. How grateful he was that his father found Pack's father so many years ago on a lonely mountain road. The boy's parents had been murdered and he'd been left for dead. *If my father hadn't brought that little Negro boy home that day, my life would've been so different now. Thank God my father had a kind heart.* He shook his head, then turned his attention back to his work.

That evening, after dinner, Jenny returned to the stable, poked her head in the doorway and called to her foreman. "Have you seen Mason? He isn't in his shop and the office is closed. I knocked, but he didn't answer."

The man laid down his rake and strode over. "I saw him earlier gathering some fishing worms and he headed for the dock behind Pack's house. Probably at the lake fishing ."

"All right, I'll try there," she said. "Thanks."

Lifting her skirt-tail, she swung around and headed down the lane. Her soft-sole shoes were no match for the stones along the gravel road. She frowned. "I knew I should've worn my work shoes," she mumbled as the rocks poked at the bottom of her feet. *It never pays to want to look like a lady.*

Several strides later, she passed the boat house. The evening sunlight reflecting on the water nearly blinded her. She held her hand to her brow to block the harsh rays. Narrowing her eyes, she caught a glimpse of Mason. He was seated on the dock with a fishing pole in his right hand, dangling his feet over the side and his back pressed against a post. Not until she stepped onto the wooden slats did he turn.

"Oh, hi," he said, straightening. Then he rose and his large frame shaded her view.

"Hi," she puffed, catching her breath. "You're a hard person to find."

"Is there something you need?"

She took another deep breath. "No, I wanted to ask you about the boy."

"Danny? What about him?" He lowered the bamboo pole and braced it against the post.

"When do you plan to bring him home?"

He tossed the remaining night crawlers into the lake and then wiped the palm of his hand on his denims. "Thought I'd go see Brad tomorrow and have him make arrangements for me to pick the boy up. He needs time to gather his clothes, toys and such. It's going to be a tough day for the young'un. "

"I'm sure," she said. "I can't imagine having to leave my home and move in with complete strangers. Poor little fella."

"Guess I'll take the wagon when I go. I'll need a way to get all his stuff home. Hopefully, I can get it in one trip."

The fishing pole gave a jerk and fell onto the dock. Mason

stomped on it, holding it tight as the line stretched out. "Sorry," he said, "I need to take care of this."

She stepped back..

He pulled in a catfish and removed the hook. "Nice one," he said, holding up the foot and a half long fish. Leaning down, he slipped it gently back into the water.

"Why aren't you going to keep it?" she asked as it swam away.

"Because I'm not much of a fish eater. I only enjoy catching them."

He dried his hands on a rag he had tucked in his back pocket, then wrapped the line around the pole and secured the hook. "That's enough for today," he said, grinning. He stared at her for a moment, then asked, "Would you care to go on a boat ride? I have a small craft inside," he said, pointing at the small building nearby. "That is if you feel like it and want to go. It's a nice evening. May be one of the last of the season. "

Her heartbeat increased two fold. "That sounds wonderful. I've never been on a boat ride before."

The corners of his mouth lifted. "You'll like it. I promise." He grasped her wrist. "You stay here while I get the craft in the water, then I'll help you in."

She smiled and nodded.

Within a few minutes, he gathered the small boat and oars, then returned. He offered her his hand and she held it tight as he helped her aboard. The craft swayed as she stepped to her seat at the front and her grip tightened. Her gaze met his and he smiled.

"It's all right. Just sit facing me and if the motion bothers you, take hold of the sides. It'll make you feel more secure. I'm not going to let anything happen to you."

She lowered onto the wood, then reluctantly released her grip on his hand.

He untied the line connected to the dock, then took the oars in hand and pushed away from shore.

Concern washed over her as the boat began moving and she whimpered a soft moan.

"You're fine," he assured her as he began rowing into the golden streaks of sunlight breaking through the trees. "Relax, you're doing fine."

A gentle breeze touched her cheeks and toyed with her emotions. The sounds of nature surrounded them. Birds chirped in the nearby trees and frogs jumped from their resting spot on the lily-pads along the shore. She took a deep breath and closed her eyes. Was this what heaven would be like? The rhythmic sounds of the oars dipping in the water added to her pleasure. All the trouble that she'd faced this past week disappeared as contentment swept through her soul. Surely she was dreaming. Nothing had ever touched her so deeply. She took a shallow breath and her eyes fluttered open. Mason, her hero, the man who'd saved her life, was there before her, now showing her a new world. She'd never felt like this before, but perhaps it took meeting the right person.

She smiled. *I think I love him.*

# Chapter Seventeen

Dusk settled over the land and Mason steered the craft onto the shore. Rising, he stepped from the boat and secured a line to the dock, then returned to help Jenny ashore. Taking her hand, he guided her out of the craft and up the bank.

"I really enjoyed the ride," she said. "I never realized how relaxing it could be."

"Glad you liked it," he said, gathering the oars.

She crossed her arms across her chest and gave a shiver. "I guess I'd better be getting back to the house. Amazing how chilly it gets once the sun goes down."

He stared at her for a moment, then disappeared into the boathouse. A few moments later, he returned with a light weight blanket. "Here," he said, placing the plaid piece across her shoulders. "I keep this here just in case it turns cool." He wrapped it around her and she grasped the corners across her breasts.

"Thank you, that feels much better," she admitted, her features brightened.

"I'll walk you home," he said, and gave her upper arm a slight tug.

The past couple of hours were the only escape she had from the turmoil that had taken over her life. She glanced at him. He was so tall and handsome. Desire pumped through her veins and her mind filled with a million questions. *I know very little about this man, yet I feel so comfortable with him. Why? I know I owe him my life, but I feel something more.* She dropped her gaze and blinked. Her eyes narrowed as she tried to focus on the stable as it came into view. Emotion ran rampant through every nerve in her body. Taking a deep breath, she hoped to exhale this compelling sensation, but it refused to budge. He was everything she'd never known in a man, yet something inside her begged to learn more. Again she glanced at him. "You're so quiet. What are you thinking?" she asked.

"Nothing," he replied, with a smile hidden behind his somber expression. She didn't need know he was smitten by her beauty. Ever since their kiss, he'd noticed a difference in her demeanor. Perhaps the boat ride stirred her emotions without him ever touching her physically. Every moment alone with her increased the desire burning in his gut. He needed her and yearned for her to have the same aching for him. Perhaps that was cruel, but he wanted this hellion tamed and in love with him. He gave her a slight squeeze. "Everything is fine. I was thinking about all that has happened lately. It's frustrating not knowing why or what to do to resolve it."

"Yes, I agree," she said glancing up. "I can't imagine why anyone would murder grandfather. He was such a kind soul."

Once again words fell silent between them. She leaned tight

against his side as they made their way along the path home… his long strides slowing to match her short footfalls. Ten minutes later, they arrived at her front door. She removed the blanket from her shoulders and turned to face him. "Thank you for such a lovely evening."

His gaze lifted over her to the dim light in the parlor. "Looks like everyone has retired for the night. Do you have your key?'

"Yes," she stated, drawing it from her skirt pocket.

"Let me do that for you," he said, and plucked it from her open palm. After struggling in the darkness to find the slot, he shoved the metal piece into the lock and pushed open the door. Turning, he gave back the skeleton key and moved aside to allow her to step past. She dropped the small object into her pocket then grasped his arm. Surprised, he stopped and gazed into her moonlit features. Gently, she placed her hands on his cheeks. Pulling his face toward hers, she pressed her lips to his. Her eyes drifted shut, then his arms folded around her and he brought her against his throbbing chest. For a long moment they embraced, then she eased away. Her eyes fluttered open and she smiled. "Goodnight," she whispered.

Speechless, he gave a nod, then she brushed past him and disappeared behind the door.

He stared at the entrance, trying to steady the passion racing through him like a bolt of lightning. A muttered curse escaped his lips as he fought back the urge to beat down the door and charge in after her. His chest clinched tight to contain his pounding heart and he swung around and rushed down the steps. ,He'd so carefully planned how to handle her and now she'd gained control of him. His unleashed emotions were overwhelmed with desire. Taunting thoughts of her kiss and the warmth of her body pressing against him sent his head spinning. "Damn it," he sputtered as he trekked along the path home. "I need to be in control. Not her. There's no way I'm getting married before I'm thirty. Not to her., Not to any woman." Arriving home, he lunged onto the porch, unlocked the door and rammed his way into the office. *I'll be damned if she is going to change my mind. I knew her beauty would challenge my judgement. I must be careful.*

He tossed the keys on his desk and head up the stairs to his apartment. There were other things to be concerned about without getting involved with a woman. *He snorted a grunt, then flipped out the light. I need to focus on the problems at hand.* With that sealed in his mind, he stumbled over and fell across the bed.

No more than five seconds later, her image appeared in his tortured mind and he squeezed his eyes tight. "Sonofabitch," he grumbled, then grabbed the pillow and covered his face. *Maybe I should've let her drown.*

Daybreak could not come soon enough. Golden streaks of sunlight crossed the room and Mason sat up on the bedside, then shoved his fingers through his hair. He could not remember a more miserable night. Jenny had branded his brain with her beauty. She was all he could think about, no matter how hard he tried to resist. Grumbling, he stood, then strode to the washbowl and pitcher on the chest of drawers. He splashed the cool water in his face, then wiped it dry, all the while remembering the lavender scent of her hair next to his shoulder. He glanced in the mirror behind the chest as he released the buttons on his shirt and yanked it off. One step sideways and he tossed it across a nearby chair, then returned.

He stared into the mirror. "What the hell have I got myself into?" *I've only been in love with one woman in my entire life and she married a man and moved to Florida. My heart has been empty ever since. Damn that bastard anyway for taking her away from me.*

He dropped the towel beside the washbowl, then pulled a clean shirt from the top drawer in front of him and shoved his arms through the sleeves. Once dressed, he headed out for the day. Perhaps some time away from her would help clear his mind. He glanced up the drive. She was not there. It was much too early for her daily visit to the stable. On a satisfied sigh, he saddle Midnight and left for town.

There was much to do that day. Number one, he needed to see Brad and tell him the good news about giving Danny a home.

He adjusted the reins between his fingers, then tapped his heels against the horse's sides and turned onto the road to Lexington. Surely this would help him focus on something other than Jenny.

Mason arrived at the sheriff's office a little before ten. He tapped his knuckles against the door and a deep voice answered. "It's open, come on in."

The hinge on the wooden panel squeaked as he shoved the door aside and stepped inside. His gaze met the deputy's stare. "Is the sheriff here?"

"Nope," the husky man replied. "Gone out of town for a couple of days. What can I do for you?"

"I need to speak with one of your prisoners. Brad Collins."

The man shuffled his feet as he rose from his chair, then walked over and picked up the cell key.

A slight motion of his hand toward the adjoining room and Mason followed. "Brad, ya got company," the man grumbled as he unlocked the iron door.

"Mason," Brad said with a grin. "I was hoping to see you." He stood and shook his friend's hand.

"Ya got fifteen minutes," the burly man said as he locked the door and sauntered away.

On a heavy sigh, Mason locked his sight with Brad's. "Any word about your trial date?"

He nodded. "Sheriff said Tuesday next week at one o'clock. Can't say I'm looking forward to it."

"Well, at least you'll know what time you'll be facing."

Brad shook his head, "I still can't believe everything that's happened. I miss my wife, I miss my boy. And now I'm gonna spend most of my life in some filthy prison. All this because I wanted to help my precious woman get well. If Doc would've just given me the medicine until I could bring him the money, then everything would've been different." Tears welled in his eyes. "I miss them so much. Don't think I'll ever get over losing my darlin'. And Danny…he'll be grown by the time I get out."

Mason placed his hand on his friends shoulder. "Listen to me.

Everything's going to be fine. Maybe you won't be in as long as you think. Also, I came to tell you I'm going to take the boy home with me."

"You are?" he said, dragging his shirtsleeve across his cheek to catch a fallen tear.

"Yes, the couple who are servants to the woman next door said they would help me care for him. They lost a child of their own and said they would be delighted to care for him while I work. They are good people. I promise we'll do our best to look after him and see that he goes to school just like you planned."

"Oh, my God, that's wonderful," he said, grasping Mason's upper arms. "I'll get word to my neighbor and have her gather his things. Is it all right if he brings some of his favorite toys? He'll need something to play with."

"Sure. In fact, let him bring that kitten he loves so much. That will give him something to hold and love. I know how important animals are to little ones."

"That'll be great. Thank you so much. I really appreciate this."

"How about I come in on Tuesday when the judge is here, then on the way home I'll stop by and pick up Danny."

"All right. I'll make sure he'll be ready."

Mason stepped back and called for the deputy, then turned back to Brad. "You stop worrying. Everything's going to be fine."

Brad nodded as the husky man swung open the door.

"See you Tuesday," Mason said, brushing past him and moving into the hallway.

Wrapping his hands around the bars, Brad smiled. "Thanks, Mason. I'll never forget this."

Mason glanced over his shoulder and gave a quick wave, then disappeared from view.

"You're a great friend and wonderful boss," Brad whispered, then flopped back on the cot and folded his arms above his head. "Thank God there are a few good people left in this world."

# Chapter Eighteen

Jenny scurried down the back-porch steps and headed for the stable. Sunlight washed her shoulders as she shuffled through the small clusters of fallen leaves. Autumn was always such a beautiful time of year. The golden tones painted a masterpiece across the landscape and she scanned the countryside drinking in the vista. Winter would soon be upon them and nature bowed her head, making way for the new season. How amazing to watch life's miracles perform before your very eyes. She stopped for a moment at the opening to the private path and stared. So few take the time to enjoy the world and all the simple pleasures it offers. Perhaps the boat ride had opened her eyes to nature's gifts. Or was it Mason? A smile broadened her features and she continued her trek to the stable.

Ten minutes later, she approached Mason's office building and glanced through the front window. By this time, he was usually busy in the workshop, but she could not resist trying to catch a glimpse of him, if he'd been delayed. After all, he could very well be at his desk doing paper work. She lifted up on her tiptoes. Nope, he was not there this morning. The room was dark. Disappointment leveled her stance. Shrugging her shoulders, she continued across the road to the stable.

The rattle of buckets and the scrape of shovels, along with all the scents of a working horse barn, greeted her. She eased past a worker pushing a wheelbarrow full of manure and turned away, hoping not to inhale the offensive odor. Once past, she spotted her foreman and stepped over, touching his shoulder to grab his attention.

He turned with a jerk, then smiled. "Hi, Miss Jenny." The dark haired man hung the halter he was cleaning on a nearby hook, then straightened. "Did you see our new sign?" he asked, stuffing his fingertips into his denim pockets. "Sure is a nice one."

"No, not yet," she replied glancing behind him at the open gate on Midnight's stall. "I came the back way."

"Well, it's a real beauty," he said, widening his grin. "Anyone passing this way will be able to see it from quite a distance. Sure looks great sitting high on those handsome stones. It fit right in where they took out the Crystal Falls sign. What ya gonna do with it now it's down?"

"I'll have them take it over to Mason. He can decide what he wants to do with it."

The man nodded. "Good idea."

"Speaking of Mason, have you seen him this morning?" she asked, gesturing toward his horse's empty stall.

He stepped sideways to allow a worker past. "Oh, he left early this morning. I passed him on my way to work. Said he had business in town."

She nodded as she recalled their conversation about Danny and knew that Mason was anxious to tell the boy's father the good news. Her thoughts tumbled back to the business at hand. "Be sure to have that extra stall clean and ready for our visiting mare this week. We want her to be most comfortable during her stay. After all, she'll be meeting the father of her next foal and we want her to enjoy her visit."

He laughed. "I don't know about her, but I'm sure Ibn will be excited."

She punched his upper arm. "You men are all alike. You all think the same." On a giggle, she swung around and headed out the door.

As planned, she gave three of her show horses a day of not only exercise, but a complete run-thru of their particular specialty. Even Ibn was groomed and put through his routine for an upcoming show. About four that afternoon and nearing exhaustion, she stopped at the well for a cool drink from the community dipper. She was never too proud to put her lips to the same cup her workers used. She worked like a man and they respected her for it.

Pulling a ragged breath, she plucked her kerchief from her skirt pocket and wiped her brow. A quick thrust of the dipper back into the bucket, she lifted the metal handle just as she noticed a lone rider approaching from the main road. Her grip eased and she lowered the piece back into the water, then raised a hand to shade the sun from her eyes. The tall, well dressed stranger came directly to her and stopped. He removed the black derby that perched atop his greying hair, then drew a folded paper from inside his suitcoat pocket. "Do you belong to the Jackson family?" he asked, his voice strong and heavy with a northern accent.

"No, sir," she replied, moving closer. "You must be looking for Mason Jackson, the craftsman. He's not here right now. Could I give him a message for you?"

"Is he the owner of this estate?"

"Well, he owns a small piece of what is left of it." She wrinkled her nose and eased into the visitor's shadow. "You see, my grandfather and I purchased eighty-five percent of the property a short while ago, so you probably need to talk to me, not him." Her brows lowered. "What, may I ask, is your name and why all the questions?"

"My name is Sid Freeman and I work for the United States Government," he said as he settled his hat back into place and stepped down from his horse. Clearing his throat, he opened his palm and shoved it toward her.

She stared at the gloved hand for a moment, then clasped it. "Nice to meet you. I'm Jennifer Jones. Now, what is it I can do for you?"

He glanced sideways as two workmen rounded the corner of the building, each leading an Arabian to a nearby corral. His eyes widened as he reconnected with her stare. "Is there somewhere we can meet in private?" he asked. "I'm here on official business and my words are not for everyone to hear."

The cut of his glare gave her concern and she motioned him toward the stable entrance. "Follow me, I have an office inside. We can talk there."

Folding her fingers between the pleats of her skirt, she lifted her dress tail and proceeded to her small but well-furnished headquarters. Once inside, she locked the door behind them and gestured toward the brown leather wingback chair. "Have a seat," she said as she stopped and faced him.

"Thank you, but this won't take long," he said opening the paper he carried tight in his left hand. "I believe you should read this," he said, shoving it toward her. "This will help explain my purpose for being here. If you are the new owner, as you say, then I'm sure you are unaware of the history surrounding this property. In fact, even Taylor Jackson himself probably knew nothing that would help shed any light on this investigation."

Her stare deepened, then she plucked the two-page draft from the man's hand. Halfway down the page, she stopped and stared at him once more.

"This incident took place some thirty years ago. Why are you just now looking into it?"

"Because we have reason to believe the missing money is somewhere in this area."

"It says here there were five Union soldiers in charge of delivering the strong boxes to Louisville from Atlanta. Why don't you look up these men and ask them what they did with the money."

His brows lifted. "Because they're all dead." He pulled a deep breath, then continued. "But we do have a few clues as to what became of the bags of gold and silver."

He wiggled his fingers toward the paper, encouraging her to read more.

Just as she finished the last paragraph, she became distracted by the image outside the office widow. Mason dismounted and drew a dipper of water from the bucket perched on the well's narrow rim. She lowered the draft and rushed to the window. With a twist of her fingers she unlocked the latch and raised the pane. "Mason," she called. "I need you to come here."

He pitched the remaining water onto the ground and dropped the dipper back into the bucket. On a curse, he gathered Midnight's reins and gave them a jerk, then led the animal into the barn. Moments later, he placed the horse in his stall and then arrived at the office. Puzzled, he stepped past Jenny and glared at the stranger.

She pushed the door shut, then said, "Mason, this is Sid Freeman. He's here on behalf of the U.S. Government."

The man clasped Mason's open hand and gave a nod. "I understand your family owned all of this estate prior to this young lady's purchase."

"Yes, sir."

"Then you must be aware of the money that was hidden in this area by the Union soldiers."

Mason shook his head. "I have no idea what you are talking about."

Jenny handed him the document and he quickly scanned the two pages, then frowned at the stranger. "This says nothing about our property. It only says the money was left in an undisclosed area that covers quite a bit of this county."

"True, but during the past six months it has come to our attention that there are men known as treasure seekers who have uncovered new information and will stop at nothing to get their hands on that money. Knowing that, it's my job to find the cash first. I've come here to ask for your help. Of course, there is danger involved, but there is also a reward, if you uncover it for us."

"Maybe all the strange things that have happened lately are connected to these treasure hunters," Jenny said, directing her words to Mason.

His brow lowered and his glare cut back to the messenger. "But you're only guessing it is on our property. There's no hard evidence."

"Well, I do have something," he said, dipping his fingertips into the inside pocket of his suit coat. A heartbeat later, he pulled out a faded piece of cloth with frayed edges.

An audible gasp escaped Jenny's lips.

The man turned with a jerk. "You recognize this?"

"Let me see that," Mason said, plucking it from the man's fingertips. He held it up to the light, then his gaze shot to Jenny. "This certainly looks like it fits the piece we found on your grandfather."

The man pushed closer. "You have a piece like this?"

"I believe so. I'd have to get it to compare the two before I could say for sure."

"Then by all means do," Freeman insisted. "My understanding is that there are four pieces to this map. The four men who hid the money drew a map, then tore it into four pieces. Each taking one section so no one could go back and take the treasure without the others knowing."

Mason's stare deepened. "What about the fifth soldier? Why didn't he get a piece?"

"So I've been told, that soldier was killed just before the money was hidden. There was an ambush and brief encounter with the enemy. Realizing there were more Rebs hidden on the trail ahead of them, they hid the gold and silver, then filled the bags with stones and put them in the strong boxes."

"Clever idea," Mason said with a grin. His words fell silent for a moment, then he said. "Wonder why they never came back after the money?"

"Three of the four died a few weeks later of some kind of madness. The fourth moved to somewhere in South Carolina and was never heard from again." The man turned to face Jenny. "How did your grandfather happen to have part of the map?"

She glanced at Mason, then back to the visitor. "I believe his older brother gave it to him. Grandfather only mentioned it once when I saw him tuck it away in an old tobacco tin. He just said it was a souvenir from when his brother was in the war. He also had a silver dollar with a bullet stuck in it. Said the dollar saved his life.

He carried the piece in his shirt pocket and it stopped the bullet from hitting his heart. "

"That must be the one I found where your grandfather was murdered. I have it in my office in the top desk drawer." He glanced over to Jenny. "I think you need to go up to the house and get the piece of map from the safe. Perhaps we can get a better idea of the treasure's location."

She nodded, then scurried out the door.

# Chapter Nineteen

Mason turn to Mr. Freeman. "Why don't we go over to my office while she is gone and I'll show you the coin I have with the bullet lodged in the center? It may be of some help in learning more about this case."

"Excellent idea," the man said and followed Mason out the door.

A brief walk and the two men arrived at Mason's office. "Make yourself comfortable. This shouldn't take but a couple of minutes," Mason said.

Freeman glanced around the room, then walked over and took a closer look at a birdcage on a shelf beside a woman's photograph. "What a beautiful piece of workmanship," he mumbled, gliding his fingertips across the metal surface. This is truly a work of art." He turned to face Mason. "My wife would have a fit over such a masterpiece."

Mason glanced up. "It belonged to my mother. That's her picture beside it. We never had a bird, but she treasured it as if it were gold."

"My wife collects fine pieces like this," the man said. "You wouldn't consider selling it would you?"

Mason laughed. "No. She'd come right out of her grave after me if I did that. You see, I guess I haven't had a chance to tell you this, but before we owned this property, it belonged to our neighbor. He lived alone and, as he aged, mother would take him food and spend a lot of time just visiting with him. When he died, he left her this section of land. He also left her the yellow canary. God knows he loved that bird. So, he had this beautiful cage special made and asked her to care for it after he was gone. Anyway, his last wish was that when the bird passed, he wanted her to keep the cage as a reminder of his love for not only the bird, but for her as well. She'd become like family to him and this was the only way he knew how to show his love."

"What a nice story," the visitor said, stepping away from the piece. "About what time period was it that the old man died?"

"Mmm, I'm not real sure. It was before I was born."

"I guess there would be a record of it at the surveyor's office."

"I know he owned it during the war, 'cause mother spoke of it," Mason declared. "He told her that he was always hiding his stock from the soldiers because they would steal chickens or his cattle just to survive. Must've been some pretty hard times back then."

"So I've heard," Freeman said.

"Oh, here it is," Mason chanted, holding up the silver coin. The man stepped over and fronted him. "May I see it?"

"Certainly," Mason said, dropping the coin into the man's open palm.

Freeman strode to the window and held the piece up to the light. "Hmm," he muttered as he turned the silver coin from front to back. "This looks like a pistol bullet. I'd guess it's a .58 caliber Confederate bullet issued to North Carolina troops. It appears to have a solid base and flattened edge. Very typical of this particular bullet."

"You seem quite knowledgeable about guns and what type ammunition was used."

The man chuckled. "I have seen a few pieces over my lifetime." He lowered the coin and stared at it, then glanced back at Mason. "I believe you also have one of the silver dollars that were among those being transported west. You see, we requested these dollars have a slightly larger mint mark. If you compare this with one of your own, you'll see the difference."

"I'll be damned," Mason grunted. "Never thought about something like that."

Freeman offered a crooked smile. "That way, if they were stolen, we could easily identify them."

"So you think the money is out there in circulation?"

"Possible, I guess," he said, handing the coin back to Mason. "But I've only come across two others over the years. They were both found in the possession of one of the soldiers that accompanied the strong boxes that fateful night. It's our opinion that the four who hid the money split up some of it and hid the rest, planning to come back later to retrieve the treasure."

"If they took some, then why not take the gold? It was worth far more."

The man arched his brow. "My thought is the gold would be too obvious. The silver they could use without any questions asked. They could retrieve the gold later. "

"True," Mason uttered as he dropped the coin back into the desk drawer. "Sounds like you've given this a lot of thought."

"You have no idea," he rasped. "I've been working on this case for years. I just hope my being here will end this mystery. I'm tired of all the dead ends. If I can locate at least part of the money, I'll retire a happy man."

"Well, good luck, because I have no idea about the location nor have I ever heard anything about the incident you speak of. Surely, if the money was somewhere on our property, someone in my family would've known about it. I hate to disappoint you, but I think you've hit another stone wall."

An instant later, Jenny burst through the doorway, carrying the piece of blood-stained map in her hand. "Here," she puffed, trying to catch her breath. "Wish you'd told me to meet you here. I've been everywhere looking for you."

"Sorry," Mason said. Slipping the drawing from between her fingertips, he spread the piece open on top of the desk.

Freeman shook open his piece and eased it up against the frayed edge. A crooked smile crossed his lips and his gaze came into contact with Mason's. "Looks like a match to me. What do you think?"

"I say so," he muttered as Jenny pushed closer to get a look, too.

"But where is the rest of it," she asked, directing her gaze to the visitor.

He glanced at Mason, then back to her. "Good question. I'm thinking the treasure hunter that has been messing with you has one of the sections. He's probably trying to spook you in hopes of scaring you into selling the property. I would guess he was about to make an offer on the land when you and your grandfather purchased it."

"Do you think that was who killed grandfather?" she asked with a frown.

"My guess is yes. Your grandfather must've come across them while they were snooping around and when he confronted them, they killed him."

"I suspected they were responsible, but I had no idea why," Mason said. For a long moment, he stared at the man. "So, now you have these pieces together, do you see anything here that will tell you where the money is hidden?"

Freeman hovered over the map, then pointed at the smeared X on Jenny's piece. "I believe this marks the location, but is this north or south of the falls?"

"I'd say north and, if that's true, the mark is not on my estate. It belongs to the state of Kentucky. There once was an Indian village there and the government declared that land be held by the state in honor of their tribe."

"Hmm, interesting," the man declared. "What tribe?'

I've heard the name a dozen times, but I was just a young'un. I really don't remember. To me it wasn't important. Mother spoke of the Indians often and said on the night of a full moon their spirits would return to the falls and bless those who were present. She was a firm believer in their power and spoke of how they danced in the waters and cast their spell on those who attended the ceremony."

"Did she ever take you?" Jenny asked.

He chuckled. "No. I was young. It scared me to think of seeing ghosts."

"All right, back to the map. Is there any place over there that would be a good hiding place?"

"I'm not sure. I never went over there," he admitted.

"Well, I think I'll go back in town and get a real map of the property. We may not need the other two pieces drawn up by the soldiers," the man declared. "You lock your piece back up and I'll be back in a day or so and we can compare the state map with this one. Then maybe I'll go over and take a look around. First, I need to get permission to go on that property. The government doesn't want just anyone snooping around on their land. Especially if I need to do some digging."

Mason nodded. "Sorry I can't be of more help. I just don't know anything about the property."

Freeman straightened, then picked up his section of the map. "You've been a big help and I appreciate your cooperation. At least this gives me something to go on. It's the first solid lead I've had in some time."

Mason shook Freeman's hand, then the man tipped his hat at Jenny and left the building.

She picked up her piece of the map, then glanced up. "Goodness, Mason, what do you think?"

"Looks like we have a real mystery on our hands."

His eyes widened. "I know one thing, if it's true there is money hidden nearby, we've not seen the last of those treasure hunters. I'm sure they'll do whatever is necessary to find that stash before Mr. Freeman finds it."

"But he said there's a reward if they find it and turn it in."

Mason snickered. "They aren't going to settle for a reward when they can have the whole thing for themselves. Believe me, these men are willing to do whatever it takes to claim the whole amount. They've already killed your grandfather. They aren't going to bat an eye if they have to kill again. This has already turned out to be far more involved than I'd expected. We're going to have to be careful about what we say. Don't need anyone else joining in this treasure hunt."

"Do you think we're in danger?" she asked, following out the front door.

"Of course we are." He locked the door to his office and accompanied her to the stable. "Don't mention this to any of your workers. The fewer who know about this, the better off we'll be. We just need to keep our eyes open and hope for the best."

She nodded as he guided her through the stable doorway. "Were you able to see Danny's father today?"

He broke open a bale of hay and carried it into Midnight's stall, then picked up a metal bucket as he returned. "Yes. I'm going to bring Danny home Tuesday after the judge sentences Brad. At that time, I should have some idea how long we will need to keep the boy."

"Are you still planning on taking the wagon to bring home his things?" she questioned, following him out to get Midnight.

"Guess so," he said as he gathered the reins and led the horse back into its stall. He unsaddled the Morgan, then grabbed a brush and began grooming the animal. "You have a better idea."

"Maybe," she said, with a slight giggle. Folding her arms, she rested her weight against the gate. "Would you consider letting me go along and help bring the boy home? We can take my open surrey. It will be more comfortable and perhaps make the lad feel more at ease. That way, we can get to know one another. Women do have more of a way with children than men do, you know."

He glanced over the horse's back and smiled. "How can I say no to such an offer? But, we will need to be there early."

"I'll be ready whenever you say," she said, straightening.

A moment later she turned to leave, then fronted him once more. "Oh, by the way, Agnes is fixing a baked hen for dinner tonight. Would you care to join us?"

"I love baked chicken," he said and his smile widened. "What time?"

"Seven will be fine," she replied with a sheepish grin. "Don't be late."

He gave a nod and a wave as she hurried out the door.

# Chapter Twenty

After dinner that evening, Mason held the front door open, allowing Jenny to pass. She stepped over to the rail on the veranda, then turned to face him as he strode toward her.

He gave his stomach a slight rub. "My, that was a wonderful meal. I ate way too much. And the baked apples were absolutely delicious. Were they off the trees out back?"

"Yes, they produced a lot of wonderful apples. That's something we never had much of when we lived back east." She swung around and faced the flagstone path up to the front steps. "It's a beautiful night. Would you care to go for a walk?"

He eased up behind her and placed his hands on her shoulders. "Not a bad idea," he said, his fingertips touching the locks of her long hair resting between his hands. "Do you need a wrap?"

"No, I'm comfortable," she said, glancing up at him. "The long sleeves on my dress will keep me warm. Besides, we won't be gone that long."

Clutching her arm, he helped her down the steps and they strolled along the walkway and onto the lane leading to the main road. Crickets and katydids grew quiet as they passed the nearby pasture. He slipped his hand down her arm and locked his fingers between hers. A smile crossed her lips and she pressed closer to his side.

"I enjoy being with you," she said, her voice soft in tone. "I feel I've really come to know you these past few days."

"Well, I like getting to know you, too," he said, not admitting the reservations he carried within his heart. She was charming and beautiful, but he wanted no part of a lasting relationship with her or any woman at this point in his life. True, he wanted to make love to her, but would she agree to such an affair without a commitment on his part. Perhaps...at least it would be worth a try. He pulled her to a stop, then lifted her hand and kissed the top of her fingers.

She raised her free hand and pressed her palm to his cheek. His lips sought hers and she wrapped her arms about his neck. With heart pounding, he drew her against him and gave her a deep and caressing kiss. The warmth of her response sent passion racing to his groin. Damn, he wanted her. "Let's go to my place," he whispered.

"I-I don't know," she stammered. "I-I've never been with anyone before."

"If you'd rather not," he rasped, his words tumbled like rocks in his throat.

She stared at his moonlit face, then tiptoed and kissed him again. "Yes, let's go to your place."

He swept her up in his arms and she pressed her cheek against his shoulder. The lavender scent in her hair filled his nostrils and enhanced his desire, but the flame burning inside him would not be a lifetime commitment. As delightful as she felt in his arms, he knew this would only result in heartbreak for her.

"Are you sure?" he asked, adjusting her weight in his arms.

She nodded.

He kissed her once more, then swung around and headed for his apartment. Upon arrival at his office, he unlocked the door and stepped inside. With muscles aching, he tightened his embrace, then kicked the door shut and carried her up the stairs. Impatience lengthened his steps and his boot heels scuffed the wood floor as he crossed the room and gently lowered her onto his bed. Moonbeams splashed through the nearby window and settled in an array of shadows, adding magic to the moment. Jenny's golden hair splayed above her head crowning her features like the goddess he'd always dreamed of conquering. He took a deep breath, then slid onto the mattress beside her. A smile creased his lips as he pushed aside long strains of her hair that had settled beside her neck. His heart rammed against his chest as he nibbled along her tender neck, then blew soft puffs of breath into her ear.

A deep moan erupted from her throat and she squirmed, then snuggled closer, begging for more.

His body responded with an immediate throbbing within his groin. "Roll over," he whispered. On a deep sigh, she did as he asked and he began unfastening the buttons on her dress.

Moments later, he separated the silk-like material and proceeded to unlacing her corset. Each touch of his hand against her flesh sent his desire spiraling to greater heights. His lungs begged for air as his body tensed in anticipation. Then the moment arrived. He reared back and his mouth flushed dry as he spread the corset wide and her young breasts came into view. Beautiful, just as he expected. He could not resist touching them. His hands massaged their tenderness and then he lowered to taste the bud-like tips of her nipples. Instantly, lust swept in as he savored the sweet flavor of her flesh.

She moaned once more.

In wild anticipation, he rose from the bed and began undressing. Never taking his eyes off her, he watched as she wiggled out of her dress and removed her underskirt. He kicked off his boots, then unbuckled his belt and opened his trousers.

Suddenly, an unfamiliar noise grabbed his attention. He lowered his brows and glanced at the window. *What the hell was that?*

He shoved the button back in place and closed his pants. Huffing, he rushed to the window.

"What's wrong?" she asked, locking her fingertips on the waistband of her pantaloons.

"I'm not sure," he replied. Flipping the latch open on the window he pushed the glass aside and stuck his head through the opening. "I smell smoke," he said. Narrowing his eyes, he scanned the landscape. A flickering orange light caught the corner of his eye. Concern bit at his emotion and he leaned farther out the window. The glow increased. He held his breath and stared at the north edge of the building. "Ah, shit," he shrieked.

"Please, tell me what's wrong?" she pleaded, rushing up behind him; her clothing still scattered across the bed.

He pushed her aside and snatched his shirt from the floor and rammed his arms in the sleeves. "I think my workshop is on fire."

"Oh, no," she gasped.

Sucking a breath, he snapped two buttons on his shirt, then tucked in his shirttail. "I've got to go," he rasped.

"No, wait. I'm coming too," she yelled. He ignored her words and dashed down the stairs. His only concern was his materials in his shop. Frantic, he shoved his way through the office door. His eyes widened as he rounded the building and the workshop came into full view. He swallowed hard.

Every tool he and Pack owned was in that building. Flames lapped from the broken window and up the wooden exterior. Mason's heart lurched in disbelief. His whole life was burning before his eyes. How the hell could this be? He held up his arm to protect his face from the heat as he edged closer. The orange-red blaze spread across his work bench and ate its way up the walls. Even his latest project was being consumed by the fire.

He gulped, then swung around and rushed to the well.

Jenny caught up with him just as he thrust the bucket into the water.

"What can I do?" she yelled, gasping for another breath.

"Get the other bucket by the rain barrel," he shouted. "Fill it and bring it to me," he huffed, jerking the full container from the hook and line. Water splashed across his pant leg as he dashed back to the burning building. Edging as close as he dared, he lifted the container and tossed the water into the flames. Smoke and embers lifted into the sky and disappeared, but made little impact on the raging fire.

Disappointment swept through him and he lowered the bucket.

An instant later, Jenny touched his arm. On one last glimmer of hope, he took the pail and slung it onto the nearest flames. It responded with a hiss, then a rush of smoke and embers twisted up and away.

A crushing wave of defeat overwhelmed him and he lowered the container. "There's no use fighting it," he muttered. His shoulder shrugged, as the heat intensified and a curtain of flame consumed the building. Stepping back, he guided her away from the inferno. "I can't stop it. It's too far gone." A moment later the roof collapsed and the burning wood lit up the entire area. The structure reverberated like thunder as it came crashing down. Sparks and charred wood scattered in all directions.

Devastated, Mason squeezed his eyes shut and lowered his chin. A moment later, with tears blurring his vision, he surveyed the catastrophe. His lifelong dream…shattered, now lay before him in a pile of rubble. He swallowed to force down the lump in his throat, then glanced at Jenny's solemn features.

Their eyes met. He recognized the pain in her gaze and realized she, too, felt the weight of his loss. She tightened the grip on his arm. Soft sobs escaped her lips and she pressed her head against his shoulder. "I'm so sorry," she whispered.

Overcome with emotion, Mason stood wrapped in silence, trying to grasp the gravity of the moment. How, why and what had happened that caused this catastrophe? He pulled a ragged breath. *What the hell do I do now?* He shook his head, then glanced at Jenny once more. "Thanks for trying to help," he said.

She nodded.

He took her hand and started toward the private path. "I think it best I take you home," he said. "I'm sorry this ruined our evening. We'll get together another time."

"Yes, it started out so well," she said, lowering her chin.

Before they could reach the gate, the sound of approaching horses grabbed his attention. He released her hand and whirled around. The image of a rider appeared in the light of the smoldering fire. Mason squinted and immediately recognized the large pinto carrying the man dressed in black. *It's the treasure hunter. What's that sonofabitch doing here?* "Hey, you," he yelled. Stepping out of the darkness, he came to a halt in front of the rider. "Who the hell are you?"

The man gave a deep, gravely laugh. "I'm your worst nightmare."

"What are you doing on my property?"

"I'm here to claim it as my own," he said, laughing once more.

"The hell you say. This is my property and there's no way in hell you're getting it."

"We'll see about that," the man said, moving closer.

Mason narrowed his eyes hoping to get a better look at this villain. Dark eyes stared back at him and the man's pitted complexion was partially covered by a red bandana. Mason glanced into the flickering firelight, expecting to see the scoundrel's companion. There was no sign of him.

"Most of this land belongs to me," Jenny said, stepping up beside Mason. "Now you get out of here before I have you arrested."

"Oh...I'm so afraid," he snickered. An evil laugh erupted from beneath the scarf, then he leaned forward and rested his hands on the saddle horn. "You are adorable, but not very convincing." His glare returned to Mason. "You have one week. You can either sell me this property or you will die. It doesn't matter to me one way or the other." His glare cut to Jenny. "That includes you, too, young lady. It would be such a shame to waste such beauty because of a stubborn ego. In fact, I may want a taste of you myself, before I cut your throat."

Mason's lips seamed tight and his jaw clamped shut. On a deep growl, he jumped at the man. Rearing back, the scoundrel jerked his foot from the stirrup and rammed the heel of his boot into Mason's shoulder. The force caught Mason off guard. He heard a crack and a firestorm of pain streaked up his arm, then he tumbled to the ground.

Jenny rushed to Mason's side as he groaned and rolled from side to side in agony.

The man straightened in the saddle and gathered the reins. "Remember... you have one week. Don't be stupid. Sell me the property and you can go on with your lives." He slapped the horse with the leather straps and disappeared into the night.

# Chapter Twenty-One

The next day, Mason arrived home from seeing the doctor. He eased from the saddle and led Midnight into the stable. He gritted his teeth as he released the strap beneath the horse's belly and slid the saddle from the stallion's back. Each move brought more pain and he dropped the leather gear onto the ground. On a curse, he grabbed the tip of the wool saddle-blanket and tossed it aside. Exhausted, he glanced around for a place to sit, then sank onto a nearby bale of hay.

Approaching footfall snagged his attention and his gaze cut to the entrance. Jenny waved as she strode toward him. "Wow, look at you," she said gesturing at the sling on his arm. "So you went to the doctor. What'd he say? Is it broken?"

"He said my collar bone is probably cracked. The only thing he could do for me was wrap it and give me medicine for the pain. He said it'll take a few weeks to heal. I'm not supposed to use my arm for a week or two." He shook his head. "I can't do that. I have to clean up the debris from the fire. Damn it, anyway."

She settled on the hay next to him, then placed her hand on his. "Don't worry about hauling off that mess. I'll have a couple of my workers take care of it."

Before he could respond, her foreman pushed through the side door and plucked a lead rope from the row of hooks by the tackroom.

"Are you ready for Ibn?" she inquired as the man started down to corridor.

He stopped and faced her. "Yes, I have the mare in the corral out back."

"Is her owner still here?" she asked, rising.

"No, he went on into town. Said he wanted to get a room at the hotel and he'd pick her up in a couple of days."

"That's good," she said. Her gaze cut back to Mason. "Is there anything I can do for you? If not, I'm going with him for the breeding."

"Go ahead. As soon as I put Midnight in the pasture, I'm going to lie down for a while. Besides, I need to take the medicine doc gave me."

Mason watched them leave, then put away his gear. As he gathered Midnight's reins, the echo of Jenny's voice and the heavy thump of hooves warned him of their approach. He tugged the leather straps and urged his stallion toward the front entrance. Glancing back, he caught a glimpse of the two as they led Ibn up the corridor.

Beads of sweat rolled down Mason's temple. Each step sent a hot lance of pain up his shoulder. He grimaced as he forced his horse forward. Before they could exit, the foreman opened the side door. The mare gave a loud nicker and both stallions immediately reacted to her scent.

Midnight pranced and swished his tail, answered her call.

"Easy boy," Mason shouted. "She's not for you."

The black stallion lifted on his hind legs and jerked his head, tossing Mason against the wooden stall post beside them. His breath caught and his jaw clamped shut as he absorbed the shock. Pain streaked up his arm and he released the leather straps to grab his shoulder. Losing his balance, he dropped to the floor. Everything blurred, then a snort and pounding hoof-beats echoed in his ears. He glanced toward the light of the open door. Moving figures scattered as a loud commotion erupted and he recognized Jenny's voice cascading above the others in a wave of screams.

Shaken and filled with agony, Mason staggered to his feet. He steadied his stance and weaved his way toward the partially open door. Chilling shrieks of fighting stallions reinforced his worst fear. *Oh no. I was afraid something like this might happen.*

He pulled a deep breath and shoved open the door. The two animals were engaged in a fierce battle. They bit and kicked in a wild frenzy. Each stallion wanting to claim the mare as their own.

Mason stepped into the sunlight. Jenny glanced sideways. "Do something," she yelled. "You've got to stop them."

He shook off the discomfort of his injury and focused on the muscular beasts as they dropped to their knees, then came up biting at each other's neck and withers.

Two workers nearby dropped their work tools and dashed

over to the corral to help. The taller young man opened the outer gate and grabbed the mare by the halter. His companion grabbed his hat and waved off the grey stallion and held the gate closed until they could lead the frightened mare to safety. Once they had her out of harm's way, Mason released a shrill whistle. The black horse ignored the call and laid back his ears and charged Ibn again. Mason shouted at the Morgan by name, then whistled again. The animal stopped and looked in his direction.

Both animals paused, then the foreman shuffled through the dirt and snatched up the lead rope dangling from Ibn's halter. Perspiration beaded the man's forehead as he rubbed the horse's neck.

Mason eased forward. "Midnight, come," he ordered. The beast turned his head and glanced at Ibn, then, with a snort, he approached his master. Mason grasped the broken rein dangling from the bridle, then gave the animal a quick once over. Other than whelps and a few cuts, the Morgan appeared fine.

Satisfied the battle was over, the foreman clucked Ibn forward. Jenny rushed to their side. The Arabian's nostrils flared. Breathing hard, he jerked when she touched him. "It's all right, big fella," she said, rubbing her hand across his back and rump, all the while scanning his lathered coat for injuries. Blood streamed from a gash on his left front leg and bite marks scattered along his neck and withers, but no broken bones were visible. She sighed in relief. The animal's tense muscles relaxed and she faced her foreman. "Clean those wounds and then put him in his stall. We'll try later to breed them. They need time to settle down," she said.

The foreman nodded, then led the horse inside the stable.

Jenny followed them and soon spotted Mason applying medicine to his horse's wounds. Her lips flattened as she eased up behind him and placed her hands on her hips.

Feeling her presence, he glanced up.

"What the hell happened," she huffed.

He stood and faced her. "I'm sorry. He got away from me before I could stop him," he said, placing the lid back on the bottle of antiseptic. "Is Ibn all right?"

She exhaled her anger and locked her gaze with his. "Yes. He'll be fine."

"You know I wouldn't have let this happen on purpose."

"I know," she said, feeling the pain in his somber features. "You need to go take your medicine and get some rest."

He nodded, then led Midnight into his stall.

Her hand touched his arm as he closed the latch on the gate. "Don't worry about fixing dinner tonight. Just leave the office door unlocked and I'll bring you a plate."

"I appreciate that," he mumbled, then lumbered out the door.

Six-thirty that evening, Jenny appeared in his entry to his apartment with a covered basket hanging from her arm.

The bed springs rattled as he rose from the mattress and propped the pillow behind his head. On a muffled grunt, he crossed his legs and settled into place.

She smiled and lowered the wicker basket onto the side table.

"Did you get any rest?"

"Yes," he replied, leaning over to peep beneath the red and white checkered cloth as she uncovered his meal. The aroma lifted, tantalizing his taste buds. "Mmm, that smells wonderful. Pot roast is my favorite," he said, gingerly turning to sit on the side of the bed.

"Take it easy, you're not going to starve," she teased. "Besides, I need time to move this chair and pull the table over for you," she said. Lifting the oil lamp, she skimmed her gaze across the room to find a place to rest it.

Grimacing, he pointed at the chest of drawers. "Put it there by the wash bowl."

With a nod, she stepped past the rocker and carried the light across the room. Her eyes widened as she pushed aside a few scattered coins to make room for the lamp. Hesitating, she took a closer look. Amidst the change laid a silver dollar with a bullet incased. She then lowered the light onto the chest of drawers. Her gaze shot to Mason, then back to the small stack of coins. Excitement peppered through her vein as she clasped the silver dollar between her fingertips. She held up the piece, then spun around and stared at him. "This is grandfather's lucky coin," she stated.

He glanced up. "Yes, I had it in my pocket. I planned to give it to you today, but with all that happened earlier, I forgot." A smile lifted the corners of his mouth. "Go ahead... take it. You should have it...not me. Maybe it'll bring you good luck one day."

She closed her palm and drew her hand between her breasts.

"I miss him so much," she whispered. For a brief moment her eyes drifted shut, then she blinked. Her gaze cut to Mason. He'd emptied the basket and tucked the cloth beneath his chin.

"I'm sorry," she said and stuffed the coin in her pocket, then rushed to his side. "Here," she said, snatching up the basket. "Let me get that out of your way." She swung around and sat the container on the foot of the bed, then pulled the rocker across from him. Breathing heavily, she slid into the chair. "Can you manage all right," she asked as he lifted the fork and stabbed at the chunk of beef.

He pulled back the fork and his gaze lifted. "I guess you could cut the meat for me." He wiggled his fingers sticking from inside the sling. "I can't seem to be able to use this hand."

She smiled, then picked up the utensils and divided the roast into small pieces. "There," she said handing him back the fork. "I believe you can manage those."

He took a bite then muttered,"Mmm, wonderful. That Agnes is such a good cook."

"Yes," Jenny said as she pushed back in the chair and began to rock. Her gaze focused on his handsome features. Just being alone with him sent her into a maelstrom of emotion. In the short time she'd know him, he'd captured her heart. How could this be? There'd never been any other man in her life that melted the walls of her resistance. Why was he different? He wasn't dashing or charming. He was strong, proud and true to his beliefs. A smile crimped her lips. Perhaps I see a reflection of myself in him.

He glanced up. "What?" he asked, placing his fork beside the empty plate.

"Nothing," she replied. "I was just thinking."

He straightened, then eased back on the pillow. "About what?"

A slight giggle escaped her lips. "You. You're always so quiet. I hardly know anything about you."

"That's a good thing," he said, wiping his lips on the checkered cloth. "The less you know the better off you'll be. I may be a mad killer, then you'd be afraid of me."

"I doubt that," she said. "I haven't seen your picture on any poster recently."

"Truth is, I'm a very private person. I don't want everyone knowing my business."

A moment later, she stood and placed the soiled plate and utensils into the wicker basket, then put the lamp and table back into place. Inhaling, she faced him and their gaze met. Her heart ratcheted up a notched. "Let me fluff your pillow before I go," she said, reaching for the cushion behind his head.

She leaned forward and his hand banded her wrist. Her breath caught and he peered at her. "Thanks for the dinner," he said.

Pulling away, she once again reached for the pillow.

He placed his hand on her cheek, then eased it to her neck and buried his fingers in her hair. "Kiss me," he rasped.

His words sent a firestorm of passion through her and their lips met in unison.

Her eyes opened and she started to move away.

"Don't go," he whispered. "Stay. Just lay here beside me and keep me company."

She stared at him for a long moment, then lowered onto the mattress.

# Chapter Twenty-two

Impatience gnawed at Jenny and she glanced at her time piece. Two-thirty. What was taking so long? Mason had joined Brad and the sheriff at the courthouse over an hour ago. Surely the case was not that complicated. On a huff, she adjusted her back against the surrey's cushioned seat. "Come on," she whispered beneath her breath, "it's getting late and we still need to pick up the boy and gather his things." Perhaps accompanying Mason was not such a good idea after all. There was much to be done at home. She released a heavy sigh.

Movement caught her eye and she glanced sideway. A young couple holding hands came strolling by and upon eye contact she acknowledged their smiles with a nod. *How delightful. Love is such a precious thing.* Her eyelids slid shut and her thoughts tumbled back to the previous night. Every moment with Mason was like a gift. How lucky she was to have him in her life. Never having had a real beau, she was unaware of what true love really was. Sure, she'd gone to social events with young men, but nothing serious, at least not in her estimation. Anyway, there'd never been anyone like Mason. He fulfilled her every dream. Tall, well built, handsome…

how could she ask for more? And last night, just to have him ask her to stay proved, in her mind, that he cared. She only wished he'd not been injured. Their time together could've been so much more. Even the night of the fire, the flames not only destroyed his workshop, it snatched him from her arms. Was there no mercy for her love of this man?

Frustration swept in and her eyes fluttered open. Unaccustomed to idle time, she adjusted her position once more, then she stared at the main entrance. The unique structure gleamed in the sunlight and her gaze deepened. *I wonder if this is the doorway Mason spoke of building about the time we bought the estate. It's beautiful. I've been sitting here all this time and never realized the possibility. I know he's a great craftsman, but this is outstanding.*

At that moment the door swung wide and he came hustling down the steps. He untied the mare from the hitching post, then climbed onto the seat beside her. "Sorry," he puffed, guiding the horse onto the main thoroughfare. "After the judge finished, I needed to speak to the sheriff. I had to tell him about the man burning down the shop and his threatening us. Something has to be done about that bastard."

"What did he say?" she asked, holding onto the railing as they turned the corner.

"Just that he would look into it," he replied. "I told him, too, about Sid Freeman and that he also thinks this stranger killed your grandfather. It seems everyone wants to find money on our property that I've never heard about."

"Are you sure no one spoke of it? Perhaps you were so young you didn't understand."

"Maybe so. Hell, I don't know. I wish they'd just leave us alone." His brows lowered. "Our lives have been destroyed by all this nonsense." Concern creased his forehead. "I've ruined Pack's life, as well. He'll be devastated when he hears that his tools, the workshop…everything, it's all gone. He depended on me to protect his things and now there's nothing left. Gone. I don't know what to say when I face him."

She placed her hand atop his. "It's been a nightmare, but somehow we'll get through this. I know we will."

His gaze met hers. "You really think so?"

She smiled. "I know so."

Words fell silent between them.

Moments slipped by, then Jenny said, "You haven't mentioned what happened in court. Did your friend get sentenced?"

"Yes, the judge gave Brad fifteen years in prison."

"Oh, no."

"No need to fret," he said, tapping the horse's rump with the whip. "It's done and there's nothing that will change it."

Jenny corralled her concern and focused her thoughts on the young boy. Having a young'un in in her home was going to be a life changer. Perhaps she spoke too quickly when she offered to take in the child. Having had no siblings, she knew little about children. But one thing she did know was that boys were rough, rowdy and very unpredictable. This would not only be a whole new world for

Danny, but for her, too. She straightened and pulled back in the seat. Well, whatever, she was certain things would be fine. After all, Agnes and her husband knew how to handle a boy his age. That, in itself, made her comfortable with her decision.

A half-hour later, Mason halted the mare in front of Brad's home. The neighbor lady stepped onto the front porch. "Been looking for you," she said, offering a smile and fluttering her kerchief as they walked up to meet her. "Danny has his things packed and ready to go."

The lad appeared in the doorway then darted back inside.

"Danny," the grey haired woman called, as she stuffed her hanky back into her apron pocket. "Get your things. Mr. Jackson is waiting." Her wrinkled cheeks gathered to each side and her smile revealed a missing lower tooth.

Mason glanced away to keep from snickering.

Unaware of his reaction, she continued to chatter. "He's been looking forward to you coming to get him. He thinks he'll just be visiting for a few days. I didn't have the heart to tell him different."

"May I go in and help him?" Jenny asked. "I'd like to visit with him a bit before we take him away."

"Sure," the old woman said. "He's a good little fella. Sure sorry this happened."

Mason stood back as Jenny passed and disappeared inside. On a heavy sigh, he turned to the lady once more. "Brad said he gave you the key to the house."

She nodded.

"The judge sentenced Brad to fifteen year in prison, so lock the place up after we leave. I'd appreciate it if you'd come over once in a while and make sure everything is all right. If someone knows the house is empty they may try to break in."

"Fifteen years," she echoed his words. "That's a mighty long time."

"Brad was devastated when he heard the news," Mason said. "I'll try to see him when I can and give him an update on Danny. My hope is they'll let him out early." He stared at the woman's tear-filled eyes. "Brad said to tell you thank you for taking care of the boy. He appreciated all you did."

She pulled out her kerchief and wiped away her tears, then dabbed her nose.

Mason patted her upper arm. "You did a fine job." Lowering his chin, he backed away and glanced at the front door. "Why don't we go in and get his things. It'll take a while for me to put them in the carriage." He nodded toward his shoulder. "I can't carry much with only one arm."

"I noticed that," she said, as she followed him inside. "What'd you do?"

"Just a minor accident, ma'am" he replied. "It'll be fine in a few days."

Twenty minutes later, Mason took Jenny's hand as she stepped into the surrey and then he turned to Danny. "Ready to go?"

The lad squinted up at Mason. "What about Kitty," the boy asked.

"Oh yes," he replied with a smile. "We mustn't forget her."

"She's on the back porch," the elderly woman said. "I gave her a bowl of milk a few minutes ago. Just feed her table scraps later. She's used to that."

The lad rushed off, then a short time later returned with the fluffy grey cat in his arms.

Mason lifted them onto the back seat beside the bag of clothing, then grabbed the reins and slid onto the leather cushioned bench. He glanced at Jenny and gave a wink. "How about we head home?"

A grin widened her lips. "Yes," she said on a slight whisper.

He shifted and faced the woman. Her features grew tight as tears rolled down her cheeks. Her frail arm lifted and she waved.

A lump filled his throat, knowing the woman would probably never see the lad again. He fought back his emotion and returned the gesture, then clucked the horse forward.

That evening Mason waited for Jenny in the parlor. The massive clock in the entry chimed eight times as he settled into the leather chair near the fireplace. He'd spent so many nights in this room as a child. This would always be home no matter who owned it. His gaze skimmed the room and memories flooded his mind. The quiet evenings, as well as the bustling holidays filled with laughter and music, echoed in his mind. He pulled a soothing breath. *My how times have changed. I wonder what mother and father would think if they could see things as they are today?*

Footsteps on the staircase brought him back to the moment. He glanced up as Jenny approached and settled in the chair beside him. "Agnes is reading a story to him. So far things are going very well."

"I'm sure glad to hear that," he said reaching for his cup of coffee on the side table. "I put the cat out on the back porch. I hope she doesn't run away. Danny sure loves that cat."

"We all need something to love," she said. "It just makes life easier to bear."

He took a sip of coffee, then said, "I know, I miss my family. And I'm sure you miss your grandfather. He was a good man."

"Yes, and I hope they catch the man who killed him."

"They will. I'm sure we know who did it. It's just a matter of the sheriff finding and arresting him. He has a lot to answer for and the sooner the better." Mason slid the empty cup back on the table and stood. "Well, now that the boy has settled in for the night I guess I'll get on over to my place. I'll check with you in the morning to see how he's doing."

She came to her feet and touched his hand. "Do you need any help with anything? I can come over if you need me."

"Yes, come help me bathe," he said with a twinkle in his eye.

She gave him a slight shove. "Stop it. I'm serious."

He laughed. "No, I'm fine. I need to take my medicine. My shoulder is starting to ache. I do have some paper work I need to get done. There are people I must contact. Need to let them know I won't be open for business until I can get the shop up and running again. No idea when that'll be."

"I'll have a couple of my men come over tomorrow and start

clearing away the debris. They should be able to get it done in a few days."

He began strolling toward the front door with her at his side. "I appreciate the help. I need to get the place back in business as soon as possible." He grasped the doorknob, eased open the wood panel and stepped forward. "Don't come out. Its chilly this evening. Thank you, again, for going with me today. Things went very well. I'm sure your being along made things go much smoother."

Before she could speak, he leaned over and kissed her.

In response, she pressed against him and he pulled back. "Careful. You're hurting my arm."

"Oh, I'm sorry."

He smiled, then brushed his fingertips across her cheek. Her angelic features captivated him. Desire tugged at his heartstrings just as it had two nights before. God, how he wanted her, but it was not to be. He shunned away the beast within him, then gave her a quick peck on the lips. "Now you get inside. We'll talk tomorrow."

She nodded, then swung around and entered the house. Taken by the moment, she stepped to the nearest window and pushed aside the lace curtain, then watched as he disappeared into the night.

# Chapter Twenty-three

Mason finished his second cup of coffee and pushed the empty cup aside. He'd take care of that later. Right now, he needed to go up to Jenny's house and check on the boy. The first night in a strange place had to be difficult for Danny. Yesterday went well, but reality would soon set in and he'd miss his home. Mason's lips seamed tight and he stood, then strode from the small kitchen into his office. He stared at the unfinished correspondences he began the previous night. That was a task that must be completed. On a heavy sigh, he grasped the back of the desk chair, then caught glimpse of a horse and rider flash past the window.

A frown tugged at his brow. Long strides took him to the door and he stepped out onto the porch. "Well, I'll be damned," he said, jumping from the wooden planks. "Pack."

His friend slid from the saddle and shoved forward his hand.

Mason clasped Pack's palm and gave it a brisk shake. "I thought you weren't coming home until Christmas."

"I decided not to stay." he said shortening his grip on the reins. "Those people are too smart and high class for me. I'm just a country fella. I don't care for city life. Too fast-paced for me. Sides, I missed Rose. In fact, I even missed you," he said with a grin.

"I have to admit I missed you too, my friend," Mason said, dipping his chin as his cheeks flushed with heat.

Pack reared back a step and stared at the bandage across Mason's arm and chest. "What happen to you? Don't tell me Midnight finally threw your ass off his back?"

Mason chuckled. "No, no. I got kicked."

"By Midnight?"

He shook his head, then explained everything. As he spoke, Pack turned to face the charred wood that was once their workshop. "I told the sheriff about all that has happened. I feel sure that treasure hunter is the one who killed Jenny's grandfather, too."

Pack lifted his hat and scratched his head. "And this is all because he wants to buy this property so he can claim the money he thinks is buried on this land?"

"That's the way I see it," Mason replied. "Stupid, isn't it? No one in my family ever spoke of a hidden treasure, here or anywhere else around these parts, that I know of."

Pack settled his hat back into place, then made eye contact with his friend. "So what are you going to do?"

"I have the sheriff on the lookout for this idiot and he's going to arrest him as soon as possible. But, he's a slick weasel. He'll be hard to catch. As for the shop, soon as I get this mess cleared away, I'll rebuild. I have a little money put aside from when I sold the estate. I'll make sure all your tools and machinery are replaced. Thing's will be hard for a while, but I'll get it done."

"Sounds good," Pack said as he glanced down the lane at his home. "Think I'll get on over to my place. I'm sure it needs an airing out and a good cleaning."

"You need some breakfast before you go? I have a couple of eggs and a slice or two of bacon if you want." He gave a light chuckle. "But you'll have to fix them yourself. I got to start loading this mess on the wagon and find a spot to dump it."

Pack slipped his boot in the stirrup and swung aboard the gelding. "Naw, I had breakfast at Rose's place," he replied. The leather saddle creaked as he adjusted and gathered the reins. "I'll come back in a while and help. Don't get it all done before I get here," he uttered with a robust laugh, then

spurred his horse forward.

Two hours later, Mason stopped to wipe the sweat from his foreheat. Working with one arm tied to his side was a daunting task. He narrowed his eyes and scanned the mound of debris. If not for the three workers Jenny sent to help, he'd be a month or more trying to do this job alone. He shoved the kerchief back into his pocket, then glanced at the stack of charred wood on the wagon. *Damn, once we get the wagon full, we'll have to take it somewhere and dump it. Double duty, I'd say.*

He rubbed his aching shoulder. Something had to give. He couldn't keep working with one arm tied to his side. Hurt or not, he had to get rid of those bandages. Frowning, he glanced at his office. Perhaps doc's pain medicine would help. He hadn't taken anything since early morning.

"Come on, men, let's take a lunch break. Meet back here in an hour," he said, crimping a smile.

The three helpers stumbled through the remains of the work

shop and into the lane. Chatting like school girls, they stomped their feet to kick the ash from their boots. Next, they removed their gloves and headed for the well to wash up.

*Good men. It's always nice to have workers that not only get along, but do good work.*

Mason strode into his office and went directly upstairs to fetch his medicine. He drew a deep breath, then swallowed the bitter remedy. One gulp and his features tightened, then he gave a hiss. "Disgusting," he said on a curse.

For a long moment, he stared at his reflection in the mirror. His eyes narrowed into slits as he focused on the soiled bandage. "Enough," he said. He gritted his teeth and ripped away the wrapping. "I'll just have to heal without it." He glared into the glass once more. "Mason Jackson, you can do this. Forget the pain and be a man." He straightened and pulled back his shoulders.

Pain streaked up his neck like a bolt of lightning. "Mmm," he groaned, squeezing his eyes shut. A moment later, he eased them back open. "Come on, big boy, you can do this," he muttered to his reflection in the mirror. "There's work to be done."

He refused to dwell on his discomfort; there would be time for that later. He wrapped his hand around the handle of the porcelain pitcher before him and emptied the water into the washbowl. After freshening up, he stepped over and plucked a clean shirt from the wardrobe. Gingerly, he slipped on the blue checked piece and snapped up the front. It wasn't his favorite, but no matter, it would soon be soiled, too.

Mason glanced up when the office door below him slammed

shut. "Who's there," he called crossing the room to the staircase.

"It's Danny and I," Jenny replied.

Mason dashed down the narrow stairs two steps at a time. "I was wondering when you'd be here," he said, puffing as he stopped before them.

"I want to see the horses," the lad said, pointing toward the stable. "Can we ride them?"

"Not today," Mason snickered. "Maybe tomorrow."

The boy grabbed Mason's hand and gave it a tug. The injured arm responded with a firestorm of pain. He grimaced and clamped his jaw tight.

Jenny glanced at his shoulder and frowned. "What have you done?" she shrieked, folding her arms across her breasts. "Doc said to keep that wrap on for at least a week, maybe two. It'll never heal if you don't do as he said."

"Don't you worry. It'll be fine. Besides, it's in the way," he said, switching the boy's small palm to the other hand. He peered down at the lad and gave a wink. "Now, why don't we go take a look at those beautiful horses?"

"Yeah," Danny cheered and began jumping up and down.

Mason shifted his gaze to Jenny. The glare in her eyes could cut through stone. He lifted the corners of his mouth into a defying grin. "Come on, Miss Jones, let's show this young man what prize-winning horses really look like."

On a huff, she unfolded her arms and followed them out the front door.

As the boy skipped along the lane toward the stable, Mason

took hold of Jenny's hand. "I want to thank you for sending the workers over to help me clean away the debris. You have a good crew," he said.

"Yes, I feel fortunate," she said. My foreman selected them. He'd known most of them for years and knew they not only worked hard, but were dependable, too."

As they chatted, a lone rider crested the hill. Mason pulled her to a halt. "We have company," he said squinting. "I believe that's Sid Freeman." He released Jenny's hand and made eye contact with her. "You catch up with Danny. I'll see what he wants."

She nodded, then scurried away.

The horseman rode up and fronted Mason. "Afternoon," he uttered as he stepped from the horse's back.

"Hello, Mr. Freeman, what can I do for you?" Mason asked, shaking the man's open palm.

"Could we step in your office? I have something I'd like to show you."

"Sure can," he replied gesturing toward the building.

Once inside, he turned to face the man. "Did you get the map showing the property lines and such?"

Freeman pulled a paper from his coat pocket. "Yes, got it right here," he said, holding the document up between his fingers. "I've looked it over carefully," he said as he unfolded the piece and spread it out on the desk. He poked his finger near the middle. "I believe this strip of land is what you own along with the forest along the river. Correct."

"Yes, sir, looks right to me."

The man then rubbed his finger over the land on each side. "So, this would be Miss Jones' property."

"Yes, that, including my place was at one time the Jackson estate."

"All right." He moved his finger to the top of the map and pointed to an area north of the river, just below what appeared to be the falls. "Then this would be the land owned today by the government that was once an Indian village?"

Mason nodded. "True, this shows the boundaries and gives the measurements of the property, but the problem is getting over to the north shore. There are high cliffs and dense undergrowth all along that side of the river. And that water is full of rocks and rapids. Jenny went to get her horse that crossed over there and she nearly drown. How in the hell are you going to get someone over there to check it out, let alone find the money? That is if there really is any buried or hidden there." He straightened and took a deep breath. "There are stones above the falls that you can step on to cross, but the water has to be low. Right now it's too high."

Freeman reared back. "Then what do you suggest?"

"Why don't we go back there and you can see for yourself what it looks like. Maybe then you'll have a better idea as to what you want to do. I don't mind you or any of your men using my lane to access the property, but, unlike years ago, there are no roads in or out of that land that I'm aware of. Maybe I'm wrong, but I really don't think so."

"All right. If you don't mind, take me back there."

Mason swung around and the pain bit at his neck and shoulder once more. "Awk," he groaned, grabbing his arm.

"Something wrong?" Freeman asked.

"Naw, just a sore shoulder. I'll be fine." He traversed the room and opened the door. "I need to get my horse. I'll meet you back here in a few minutes."

The man stepped past him and Mason headed for the stable.

Moment later, he spotted Jenny and Danny at the well getting a drink. He stopped before them as she handed the boy a dipper full of water. "I have to take Freeman back to the falls. I'll come see you when I get back.'

"Be careful," she said.

He leaned forward and patted the boy on the head. "You do as Miss Jenny says. I have to go off for a while, but I'll be up to see you before you go to bed tonight. All right?"

Danny lowered the dipper. "Promise?"

He smiled. "Promise."

Jenny pressed he hand on Mason's wrist. "If you're back in time, join us for dinner."

He leaned forward and kissed her cheek. "If not, save me a plate."

# Chapter Twenty-four

Mason turned off the lamp and eased between the bed covers. An instant later, lightening flashed, illuminating the entire area that he laughingly called his bedroom. The whole apartment was nothing more than one large room with a few necessary items. An earth-shaking clap of thunder followed and he jerked the quilt tight against his chin. He never did like storms. There was something about them that rattled his nerves. Rain peppered against the window and he rolled onto his side trying to ignore the ruckus. He needed no more anxiety in his life. When was this drama going to end? Another flash of light… another clap of thunder. He squirmed beneath the quilt then squeezed his eyes tight. The past week had tried his patience and he searched his thoughts for relief from the madness.

Another boom and the glass window rattled. He jerked forward, sitting straight up in the bed. "Damnit," he grumbled. "It's not bad enough that my arm aches, but now this." He raked his fingers through his hair. On another curse, he tossed aside the covers and pivoted onto the side of the bed. As he stared into the darkness, an image of Jenny appeared and thoughts of early evening came flooding back. He'd promised her and Danny he'd be back from the falls in time for dinner. He arrived late and found the boy patiently waiting with Jenny in the parlor. Exhaustion and pain gnawed at him to the point where he could not enjoy their company, so after dinner he gracefully excused himself and returned to his apartment.

On a sigh, he pushed forward and his bare feet brushed against the cool wood floor, then he stood and strode to the window. *I planned to get so much done today. I need to start building the new workshop.* He frowned. *This idea of hidden money is nothing more than a hoax. Freeman said he'd be back in a day or two with a couple of helpers to search for the treasure.* Mason snickered. *He's not going to find anything.*

He narrowed his eyes and pressed nearer the glass. The storm had moved on. Flashes of lightening danced in the distance. "Good," he mumbled as he shuffled back to bed. He gave the feather pillow a shake, then tossed it amongst the wrinkled cover. After a quick rub on the sore shoulder, he lowered and stretched out on the mattress. "Maybe now I can get some rest."

Next morning, after a decent night's sleep, Mason stepped into the stable and gathered his gear. As he tossed the saddle onto Midnight's back, he caught a glimpse of someone approaching. Turning, he came face to face with the sheriff. "What brings you here?" Mason inquired as he tightened the belly strap on the saddle.

"I'm on my way to Louisville and thought I'd stop in and see how the boy's doing."

"He's doing well. In fact, better than I expected." He dropped the stirrup back into place. "Jenny's maid reads a story to him every night before bed. Yesterday, I took her a couple of story books my mother wrote. And today I promised to take him with me to order the lumber for my new workshop. We're keeping him busy, that's for sure."

I see they've about finished clearing away the old building," the sheriff said, pocking a thumb over his shoulder. "What's Pack going to say when he gets home from college?"

"Oh, he's already back. Came home yesterday," Mason said as he bridled the horse. "He didn't like Atlanta or the professors with all their degrees. Pack's like me. He's just a good ole country boy. We like doing our own thing on our own time. Don't get me wrong, he appreciated the opportunity."

"I understand completely," the sheriff said with a nod. "Just like a new pair of shoes, if they aren't the right size they're not gonna fit no matter how much you like 'em." He pause for a moment, then continued, "The other reason I stopped by was to tell you about the those treasure hunters that have been bothering you."

Mason stiffened. "You caught them?"

"No. The bartender where they hang out said the weird one with the beard went up to a room with some floosy who works there. Not too long afterwards, she came out screaming. Seems the old man died of a heart attack right in the middle of their fun."

"Good Lord," Mason said, forcing back an outburst of laughter. "Well, I guess he went happy."

"I'm sure he did. She's a fine looking woman. If I weren't married, I'd consider giving her a poke myself."

"Not me," Mason said. "I don't want a woman who's been with every man in the county."

The sheriff snickered, then said, "Anyway, I also found out the one who threatened you is his younger brother. I think he's been looking after the old man since he was kicked out of a mental hospital about a year ago."

""What! Why?"

"Cause he got caught trying to rape one of the nurses. Guess he's always had a problem that way."

Mason leaned closer. "I don't give a damn about him. What I want to know is did you arrest the sonofabitch that threatened me?"

"Hell, no, I didn't hear about this until the next day." The sheriff's brows lowered. "I can't be everywhere at once. I was out at the Parker's farm 'cause someone broke in their house. But I'll still keep an eye out for him. As long as he thinks the money is here, he'll be close by. You can't get rid of those money-hungry bastards until they get what they want."

Mason cocked a brow. "Well, you'd better get him soon, 'cause he says he going to kill Jenny and me before the week's over."

"I know, I know. I'll get on it as soon as I get back from Louisville."

"You'd better."

"All right," he mumbled as he headed for the door. "I gotta get going." Without looking back he lifted a hand and waved goodbye.

Late afternoon, Mason returned to the stable with Danny riding in front in his saddle.

Jenny stopped brushing Ibn and glanced up. "Need help?" she asked as she stepped up beside them.

"Sure," he replied, removing his foot from the stirrup. "If you'll take him, that'll be great."

She nodded, then spread her arms and the boy slid into her embrace. "Did you have fun?"

Danny grinned. "We went into town after going to the lumber place and stopped at the General Store. Mason bought me some sweets and a new pair of boots." He pointed his little finger toward the saddle bags. "They're in there."

"That was nice." she said, lowering him to the ground.

He nodded.

Jenny's gaze shifted to Mason. "Did you get what you needed at the sawmill?"

His lips cupped upward as he pulled the saddle from the horses back. "Yep. Said they'd deliver the wood next Monday."

"That's great. Is Pack going to help you rebuild?"

"Said he would," he hollered as he carried the saddle to the tack room.

She spotted the grey cat sitting nearby, cleaning her paw, and turned the lad in her direction. "Look, there's Kitty. Why don't you take her up to the house and have Agnes give her a bowl of milk?

She may have a cookie or two for you, too. I could smell them baking when I passed through the kitchen earlier."

He giggled, then ran over and swept up the ball of fur and started for the door.

"You remember how to go up the back way, don't you?"

He hesitated, then glanced back. "Yes, ma'am."

"All right, go ahead. Be careful, that hill is steep in places."

"Yes, ma'am," he said and darted out the door with the cat wrapped in his arms.

Mason eased up beside her. "I think he likes you," he said, slipping his hand behind her back.

"I hope so, but I want Agnes to be the one he really cares about. She's been all smiles since he came to stay with us."

He leaned closer and pressed his lips against her ear. "How about you meet me at the boat dock around five and I'll take you for another ride?"

She jerked around and her eyes met his. Her breath quickened. "I'd like that," she said.

"Bring your wrap. It may be cool out on the water."

"Yes, yes, I will," she stammered.

Her lips begged to be kissed, but with workers nearby, he dared not take the chance of getting caught. "Don't be late," he whispered.

"No...I won't," she muttered as she lowered her gaze and stepped away.

A gentle breeze rustled the willow trees along the shoreline. It was another perfect evening for being out on the lake. Mason pulled his watch from his denims and flipped open the face. Four forty-five. Jenny would arrive soon. His heartbeat quickened. Anticipation burned in his groin as he recalled the evening of the fire when he was about to make her his. Just the thought of her exposed breast sent a tingle throughout his body.

He glanced up the lane. No sign of her yet. He stuffed his watch back in his pocket, then took the small craft from the boat house and slid it into the water. As he leaned to tie off the attached rope, footfall rustled in the rocks behind him. On a jerk, he turned and found Jenny approaching with a picnic basket draped across her arm.

"Hi," she said as she came to a halt at the base of the pier. She smile and held up the basket. "Agnes sent us some fried chicken and biscuits with an apple and cookies for desert."

"Sounds delicious," he said, holding out his hand. "Here, let me help you in. Careful, the boat will wobble with you."

"Yes, I remember," she replied grasping his open palm. Once seated, she placed the basket on the floor beside her feet.

"Ready?"

"Yes."

He poked the tip of the oar against the bank and the craft glided out on the water.

"When Danny found out where I was going, he asked to come along," she stated. "I told him no and that you'd take him another time."

"Was he all right with that?" he asked as he began to row.

"He was disappointed. His little lips puckered, but he'll be fine." Silence filled the air as the constant rhythm of the oar filled the void. Calm, tranquil, and relaxing. She sighed, then said, "I think Danny is beginning to realize he won't be going back home."

"Why do you say that?"

"When I went up to the house after work I found him sitting on the back step with Kitty in his arms. He was crying. I asked him what was wrong. He said he wanted to go home. He told me he'd had a good time, but he wanted to be with his mother and father. Big tears ran down his cheeks and he looked up at me and said, "I miss them.""

Mason shook his head. "I was afraid that would happen."

"I put my arms around him and told him I understood and we wanted to be his family for a while."

"So, how'd he take that?"

"He just pulled away and ran into the house. I peeked into his room later and he was asleep on the rug by his bed, holding his teddy bear. Then when I left to come here, I saw him in the parlor. That was when he asked where I was going and asked to come with me. I felt guilty saying no, but he seemed all right with it. It just breaks my heart to see him so sad."

"He'll get over it," he said, steering the boat back to the dock.

She glared at him for a moment. "You men are all so harsh. Why can't you show a little compassion once in a while?"

"I have feelings, but a man has to grow up and face the world. Women are all too soft-hearted. They live in a fantasy world most of the time."

"What? How dare you say that?" She folded her arms across her chest. "Take me back to shore. I don't want to boat ride anymore. Not today, maybe not ever."

# Chapter Twenty-five

The boat brushed against the shore, then Mason grasped a nearby post and pulled the craft to the pier. After securing the tether, he turned to Jenny and held out an open palm. "Give me your hand."

On a huff, she grabbed the basket handle with one hand, then clasped his hand. Standing, she stared at him for a long moment. Hurt washed her features and she drew her lips tight, locking in the anger. Sparks snapped in her eye as she passed and climbed from the boat.

Mason gathered the oars and laid them on the pier, all the while he never took his eyes off her. Heavy footfalls carried her up the planks and onto the grassy hillside. "Never expected the day to end like this," she muttered.

A grin tugged at the corner of his mouth. *I think I hit a nerve.*

He stepped onto the pier and long strides brought him close behind her. "Jenny," he said clasping her arm.

She jerked free. "Leave me alone, you, you male….egotistical bastard."

He grabbed her again and spun her around.

She dropped the basket and raised her fists. His muscles coiled and he pulled her tight against his chest. His desire for this woman burned through his veins. He set aside the throbbing pain in his shoulder and gazed into her eyes, then he covered her lips with his. She pushed to free his grip, but his kiss deepened and she responded. A heartbeat later, his lips left hers and nibbled a sizzling trail down her cheek to the arch of her neck. His heated breath forced puffs of air into her ear and her anger disappeared on a ragged groan.

He released his grip and shifted; opening the door to the boat house. "Step inside," he said, his voice rasping with desire.

She turned and entered the dark interior of the building. Only the muted light from a small back window, hidden by boxes, allowed her to find her way through the cluttered room. She glanced back at Mason as he closed the door and secured the lock. Smiling, he strode toward her and wrapped her in his arms once more.

For a moment, his eyes caressed her. Her young, beautiful body awaited his touch. "Where were we?" he mumbled, just before his mouth found hers. A long passionate kiss left them breathless. He stopped and stared at her in the misty twilight. Her breasts rose and fell at a fever-pitched pace. He removed her shawl, letting it drop to the floor, then began to open the buttons on her dress. She drew a sharp breath as he spread the linen fabric, then unlaced the corset beneath. Without prompting, she stepped back and removed the dress and undergarment. On baited breath, she took his hand and placed it on her left breast. He gently massaged the tender flesh then leaned forward and captured the nipple between his lips, caressing the tip with his tongue.

She closed her eyes and reared her head backward. Sucking a breath of air, she expelled a lust-filled moan.

Sensing her approval heightened his desire. His hands slipped down to her waist and he tucked his fingertips beneath her pantaloons, then lowered them to the floor. Retracing his journey, his palms glided up her slender legs and he savored the mounting heat warming his fingertips. On his next inrushing breath, he edged upward to her most private area, caressing her with each stroke of his hand.

A soft whimper escaped her lips.

The beast in his denims swelled as she allowed him access to her sacred treasure. He gazed at the beauty in his arms. How fortunate he was to have a woman like this. She showed no shame in offering him her most precious gift. He leaned forward and trailed his tongue up her neck and covered her mouth with his.

Moments later, he stepped back and glanced at his mother's bedroom suit stacked against the wall beside them. The mattress, covered with a blanket, lay pressed against the four poster frame.

"Don't move," he whispered, then shifted and pulled the piece onto the floor. The thump reverberated across the wood beneath their feet as he spread the blanket over the bare mattress. His breath heavy with anticipation, "Lay down," he said. As he stripped away his clothing, she removed her day shoes and stretched her nakedness onto the cover.

His eyes captured every movement as she settled into place and opened her arms for him to enter. Such an invitation he could not deny. He swallowed hard, then lowered into her embrace. The touch of her soft skin against his naked body sent his passion soaring. His hands splayed wide and explored every curve and tender crevasse he could find, all the while tasting and suckling her small but adequate breast.

Her groans intensified with each stroke of his hands, reaching plateaus she had never dreamed possible. Each breath became a gasp as she responded to his touch. The fury of the frenzy sent her body into a quivering madness, unlike anything she'd ever experienced. She pushed back to catch her breath.

"What was that?" he asked, grinning.

She sat up panting and her eyes met his.

His lips widened. "Did it feel good?"

Unsure of what to say, she dropped onto the mattress beside him.

He cradled her in his arms and gently covered her lips with his. Again, he cupped her breasts. Each soft, yet firm, and he toyed with the buds that had popped up like a cherry on a sundae. "I need you to touch me," he whispered into her ears. The warmth of his breath rippled down her neck, sending waves of goose bumps across her skin.

She groped in the fading light of evening, then flinched when her fingertips touched the hardened flesh.

"I- I can't," she stuttered.

He pressed his lips to her ear once more. "I need you to touch me, Jenny," he said, his words rippling through her once again.

"Mason, I-I…"

Gently he placed his palm over her hand and guided her to his throbbing beast. She squeezed her eyes tight as her hand closed beneath his. Heat radiated within her grip and she whimpered. Jenny had never touched a man's privates before and was beyond fear of knowing what to do.

After a moment of pure pleasure, Mason sensed her discomfort and he pulled away. "Roll over here," he said, shifting from his side.

"I'm sorry," she muttered and a tear appeared in the corner of her eye.

"It's all right," he said lifting his large frame over her. His hot breath rushed against her neck. "Give me your hand," he whispered, then his fingers slipped between hers and held it firm. He peered down at her, soaking in her beauty. Her virgin body awaited his call and the time had arrived to release the desire that raged within him. An instant later, the animal instinct emerged. The beast needed satisfaction and refused to be denied.

"I need you, Jenny," Mason grumbled from deep within his throat. His body stiffened as his knee separated her legs and he lowered, then drove his rod of life into her.

She gasped as he pushed deep and deeper inside. She arched her back, unable to denying the beast his due.

"Oh, Jenny," Mason ground out beneath a ragged breath. "Yes, yes."

The room spun around her as a whole new world emerged. The faster he stroked the more she responded, rising and falling in rhythm on a wave after wave of pleasure, each motion fulfilling her needs. Her raspy groans intensified, joining his throaty grunts of ecstasy. She marched to the beat of his drumming heart and found it to be the most rewarding event in her life.

They continued on a collision course in a race to the peak of their emotion. Then their fantasy heaven opened its doors and there was an explosion of grandeur. Mason reared back panting as she quivered beneath him.

A heart-pounding moment later, he dropped his chin against her shoulder.

"God, you're wonderful," he said, puffing each word into her golden tresses.

Her hand pulled from his and she caressed his cheek. "I love you," she whispered.

Mason leveled over her and gave her a deep rewarding kiss, sealing their relationship. Exhausted, he rolled over beside her. "You all right?" he asked, his tone as gentle as a summer breeze.

She nodded, then peered into his eyes and brushed her fingertips across his lips. "Where have you been all my life?"

He laughed. "Right here in Kentucky. This is my home and always will be, even if it is just a small piece of land. I love this place."

"But, now I own all this that was once yours." She lifted onto her elbow. "That makes me sad that I've taken it away from you."

"That's all right. I can step out my front door and still enjoy it. Everything brings back such wonderful memories. The stable, the land, and the house where I grew up…they're all here surrounding me." He leaned forward and kissed her. "And now there is you."

She lowered her gaze and her cheeks flushed a rose pink. "I'm the one who's lucky."

"Now I wouldn't say that," he said. "I'm no prize."

"To me you are," she state.

He rose and offered his hand. "Come on. Time to get dressed. It's getting cool in here. Besides, we have a chicken dinner waiting for us."

She smiled and hopped to her feet, then pressed her naked body against his. "Mmm, you feel so good next to me," she whispered, brushing her fingers through the thick hair on his chest."

He grasped her hand. "Watch it. We may never get out of here." On a grunt, he lowered and picked up her pantaloons. "Here, get dressed," he said.

She smiled, then grasped the garment. "Only because I must," she replied and began collecting the remainder of her things scattered across the floor.

Ten minutes later as they walked hand in hand up the lane, Mason noticed a woman rushing toward them. He narrowed his eyes. The woman franticly waved a white cloth. "Jenny," she yelled, then stumbled and fell.

He glanced at Jenny. "That's Agnes."

"Oh no, something's wrong," she gasped and released his

hand, then surged forward at breakneck speed.

Mason's long strides soon overtook Jenny and by the time Jenny arrived he was lifting the woman to her feet.

On sharp gulps of air, Jenny asked, "What's wrong?"

"It's Danny," she said, clamping her arm across Mason's elbow. "We can't find him anywhere."

"Where'd you last see him?" Mason queried as he help the woman steady her balance.

"In the back yard. I was out gathering the laundry from the clotheslines and he was playing nearby with that little horse you carved for him. He's always such a good little fella. Never gives me any trouble."

"Did you check his room?" Jenny asked.

"We've looked in every room in the house. I even check the closets and the hidden storage room beneath the stairs. He just isn't any place inside or outside."

"I'll check the stable," Mason said. "Jenny, why don't you take Agnes back to the house? "I'll start looking for him and let you know if I find him. He can't be too far from here. He may have just wandered off while he was playing."

Jenny nodded, then took her maid by the arm and led her away.

# Chapter Twenty-six

Entering the stable, the aroma of fresh cut hay filled Mason's nostrils. He recalled seeing the workers earlier that day delivering the bundles while on his way to the lake.

He grabbed a lantern from a nearby hook and lit the wick. Golden beams spread across the interior and several horses responded with a soft nicker. He chuckled. *The spoiled critters are asking for another cup of sweet grain.* "You've had enough," he spoke out as he trekked down the corridor, checking each stall for any sign of Danny. Nothing. Pivoting, he returned to the entrance and glanced overhead, then to the ladder. *Yes, he's probably somewhere hiding in the loft. I did that myself a couple of times; that is, until mother got wise to me.*

After a thorough search of the barn, he found no sign of the boy. Discouraged, he left the building. With lantern in hand, he checked the entire area around the stable. Still nothing. Holding the light high, he skimmed the land across the lane, then focused on the stone well. The hair on the back of his neck prickled. God forbid if he fell in there. He gulped a hard swallow, then rushed over to the well. His hand shook as he held the light over the deep enclosure. The water below reflected against the walls, but was void of any object. On a sigh, he stepped away.

"Where the hell are you, Danny?" he spoke aloud.

Frustrated, he headed for his office to get a jacket and a bite to eat. Jenny had taken the basket of fried chicken with her. Too bad, he could sure use a drumstick right now. A grin teetered on his lips. Memories reminded him that being with her was far more enjoyable than a chicken leg. He would make that trade any day, any time.

He pulled out his key and grasped the doorknob. It moved at his touch without the key. "What the... Guess I forgot to lock it," he muttered pushing the panel aside. Stepping in, he heard something and raised the light. Two gold dots the size of marbles appeared and he leaned forward to get a better look. The picture of his mother moved and Kitty eased out from behind the frame.

Mason smiled, then placed the lantern on his desk and plucked the animal from between the birdcage and the picture. He held her close, then patted her head. "You're a bad girl getting up there. If you knocked those off, you'd be in real trouble." He glanced around the room. "Where's Danny?" he questioned the furry critter. "If you're here, I'm sure he's close by."

Lowering the cat to the floor, he circled the room, then stopped and scanned the stairs and shelves along the walls. He stacked his fists on his hips. *He's got to be here somewhere. Maybe he's upstairs.* Flattening his lips tight, he headed for the staircase. Two steps up the incline he noticed Kitty pawing under his desk. He hesitated, then narrowed his eyes to see what she was after. A couple more swipes and a young hand reached out to catch her leg. The cat jerked away and leaped upon a nearby chair.

Mason smiled, then hurried over and pulled the desk chair out and shoved it aside. Lowering on one knee he spotted the lad. "There you are. We've been looking for you. Everyone's worried."

Danny pulled into a fetal position and said, "Go away. I don't like you anymore."

"Come on out so you can tell me why you don't like me."

"No. I want to go home. My real home. Mother and Papa are waiting for me."

"Well, Jenny and I are waiting, too, and Agnes is ready to read you a bedtime story. Don't you want to sleep in that big fluffy bed with your teddy bear?"

"I want my bed at home. You said you'd take me back when I finished visiting."

"But we still have plenty of things to do," Mason said, reaching for the lad. "I want to take you fishing and go on a picnic at the falls. When it gets cold and snows I want to build you a sled and you can ride down the hills. Won't that be fun? You can even help me build it if you want."

"But I want to be with Papa."

Mason eased the boy out from under the desk and gathered him in his arms. "Papa had to go away on a job. When he gets back I promise I'll take you home."

"You promise?"

"Of course, I promise." He patted the boy's back as he adjusted him on his shoulder. "Right now, let's go up and see what Agnes has good to eat. I'm starving. How about you?"

The boy nodded, then lowered his head against the curve of Mason's neck.

"Everything's going to be fine, you'll see," he assured the lad and kissed his forehead. Shifting, he grasped the lantern, then carried the boy out the door. Satisfaction in finding the lad swept through him as brisk steps carried him up to the mansion that was once his home.

The following day as Mason filled out an order for new tools and equipment, the rattle of an approaching wagon caught his attention. He glanced out the front window. A wagon carrying unstripped logs with four men perched atop pulled to a halt in front of his office. This was not the lumber he'd ordered. He wanted wood to build with, not raw logs. He rose and pushed his chair aside. On a huff, he traversed the room and swung open the door. Sid Freeman had just raised his hand to knock . Surprised, he jerked to a stop then relaxed his frown and offered the man his hand.

"We're here to take a look at that land," the man said clasping his open palm. "My men are going to make a raft to cross to the other side. I think we'll try going upstream as you suggested."

Mason nodded. "Yes, I think that would be your best bet. Just don't get too near the falls."

"No, no, we won't do that. These men are experts on such

things as rafting and clearing land."

"Great. Can you find your way back there or do you need me to show you the way?"

"I believe we can go it alone," Freeman replied.

"Just follow the lane. You should be fine. I have some paper work to do right now, but I'll come back in a bit and see how you're doing."

"Good enough," Sid said, then turned and rejoined the crew.

As Mason watched them pull away, he caught sight of Jenny heading to the stable. Her blue work dress fluttered in the morning breeze and she drew her jacket tight across her breasts. Wisps of her golden locks crossed her face and she quickly brushed them aside. He smiled. Last evening rushed into his mind. The thought of touching her naked body awakened the beast in him once more. He smiled, then lowered his gaze. *This isn't the time or place. I have work to do. Perhaps later. Yes, later will do.* He swung around and returned to work.

An hour later, he closed the office and headed for the stable. Upon entering, he spotted Jenny brushing the mare left to be bred. "Fine looking horse," he said, stepping up beside her.

"Yes, I thought I would clean her up. Her owner is returning today to pick her up. She has such good bloodlines," she stated. "She should throw a fantastic foal. I wonder if the colt will be grey like Ibn or Chestnut like her."

"Does it matter?"

"No, not really," she said, sliding the brush onto a nearby

bench. "So, what are you up to today?"

"Sid Freeman is here. He's taking a crew back by the falls to look for that cash he swears is back there. I won't believe it until I see it. Although there must be something hidden somewhere or there wouldn't be a map. Maybe they just misread the true location of it. Hell, I don't know," he said, shaking his head.

"What they really need is the full map," she said, walking the mare to her stall.

"Well, I'm sure that idiot that wants to kill us has at least one part of it."

She returned and picked up the brush. "He gives me the creeps. I wish the sheriff would catch him and put him away for life."

"It's not going to be today," he snorted. "Sheriff's in Louisville. Maybe if he'd stay on the job in Lexington like he should, he'd be able to catch that sonofabitch." He leveled his foot on a bale of hay and crossed his arms atop his knee. "Enough about that. What about Danny? Did he do alright after I left last night?"

"Yes. Agnes gave him some milk and cookies, then took him upstairs and read him a couple of your mother's books. I saw her in the hall afterwards and she said he fell asleep not long after she finished the first story. She has such a soothing voice."

"He's a good young'un. I really expected him to want to go back home before now. He should be alright for a while now."

"I hope so." She said, putting the brush in a nearby drawer.

He straightened. "Guess I'd better get Midnight saddled and get on back to see how Freeman is doing. They should have the raft together by now. I can't keep my mind on my own work for having to deal with all this other bull. I need to get the shop back up and running." He started toward the corridor, then pivoted. "If they bring my wood while I'm gone, just have them unload it where the old building stood. Pack and I'll take care of it."

"I will," she said, as he disappeared into the tack room.

An hour and a half later, back at the falls, Mason spotted Freeman walking toward the empty wagon. Mason guided his Morgan up alongside the man. "How's it going," he asked, sliding from the saddle.

"Slow, we just finished tying the logs together. It's a rather crude raft, but it works."

"Have they made it across yet?"

"Oh, yes, they're across, but not before they got caught in the current and it nearly took them over the falls. If they'd hit those boulders below it would've killed 'em all. I sure don't know how those soldiers got across there without some kind of boat. And why the hell didn't they just hide the cash on this side of the water. That was a dumb move on their part, in my way of thinking."

"Scared people do strange things," Mason said, peering across the water. He skimmed the hillside for a sign of the workers. "Where are they, anyway? I sure don't see anyone."

The man pointed to his left. "Deep in that undergrowth. See the bushes moving?"

Mason raised his hand to shade his eyes. "Now I see it. It's so thick I don't see how they can move."

Freeman laughed. "They are used to working in heavy terrane. That's why I chose them."

"Not me. I'd be so full of chiggers I wouldn't sleep for a month."

"Hey, Sid," one of the men yelled. "I think we found an old trail back here. Not wide enough for a wagon, but a horse and rider could travel it." Silence followed, then more bushes shook and the man yelled again. "There's a steep incline west…and east, it looks like. I don't know," he puffed. "I'll have to clear more, but it looks like a path."

The men chattered amongst themselves as they worked their way along the hillside. Cracking and popping noises erupted as they tore away small trees and undergrowth.

After a half hour, Mason lifted into the saddle. "I'm heading back. On your way out, stop by my office and let me know how things went."

"Sure thing," the man said. "Not much can be done here until they clear this all away."

As Mason turned the stallion, screams echoed up the valley floor.

His's eyes widened.

Suddenly, someone yelled, "Run," and the men rushed out of the thicket and ran toward the shore. "Bat's, hundreds of them," the leader shrieked, then he dove into the water.

# Chapter Twenty-seven

"Oh, no," he yelled, then jumped from the saddle and ducked beneath the wagon.

Panic shrouded Freeman's face as he hovered at Mason's side.

The vicious creatures swarmed overhead. In a flapping fury, they circled; darting and screeching their warnings.

"Cover your head," Mason shouted. "Their bite can kill you."

"I-I know," the man replied, shuddering with fear.

Moments later the dark blanket of madness lifted and disappeared into the eastern sky.

Sounds of rushing water replaced the noise and Mason eased forward, lifting his chin from beneath the front flap on his jacket. "It's all right, Sid, I think they're gone," he said, crawling from beneath the rig. Raising to his feet, his gaze swept the landscape in search of the workers. He spotted one man across the river, hanging onto a tree branch.

Freeman staggered up beside Mason. "Can you see anyone?" he asked, his voice still trembling.

"Over there," Mason said, pointing a finger. "He's on that limb trying to work his way to the shore. I don't see anyone else."

He glanced at Midnight. "I'll ride downstream and see if the others survived."

"I'll get the wagon and come too."

"No, you wait here. It's too dangerous. The riverbank is very steep in places." His attention shifted to the man across the way struggling to reach land. "If your friend there gets to the shore, tell him to get on the raft and come back over. I think you've all had enough excitement for one day."

Freeman nodded.

Mason gathered his horse's reins and swung aboard the stallion, then headed down stream. As he approached the river's bend where he pulled Jenny from the water, he caught sight of a man lying on the grass. Drawing closer, he recognized the man as one of the workers. He was breathing hard, with his forearm resting across his face.

"Hey, you all right?" Mason called out.

The man lowered his arm and shifted onto his side. He coughed a couple of times as he lifted on his elbow, then sputtered, "I-I guess... Think I swallowed half the river."

"Probably" Mason snickered, then reined Midnight up beside the worker. "Can you get up or do you need help?"

"I'm all right. Just give me a minute to catch my breath," he muttered. A moment later, he sat up, then ground out another fit of coughing. On a moan, he heaved up a mouth full of water, then stumbled to his feet. "Damn," he growled. "What a ride."

"Yep, those rapids are pretty tough," Mason declared as he

removed his foot from the stirrup. Holding out an open palm, he said, "Climb aboard. I'll give you a ride back."

The man clasped his hand, then pulled up and leveled onto the back of the saddle.

As Mason gathered the reins, a cry for help cut through the air. He jerked Midnight around and narrowed his eyes. In the distance, he noticed a man standing, waving his arms. A grin widened his lips, then he dug his heels into the horse's sides and they surged forward.

Minutes later, he halted the stallion beside the worker. Streams of blood tracked down the man's forehead from a gash just below his hair line. An instant reminder of Jenny's injuries swept through his mind. "You all right?"

The man mumbled and nodded, then pressed his wet shirtsleeve against the wound.

Mason leaned forward and drew a bandana from his pocket and pitched it to the man. "Here, use this and hold it tight against that cut. That should stop the bleeding." The workman grunted and snatched the cloth from his hand. "Soon as I take your buddy here back to the wagon, I'll come get you." He glanced around then pointed. "Lay down over there and rest until I get back. Don't want you passing out."

The dazed worker nodded once more, then Mason swung the horse around and bolted forward.

Once everyone had gathered safely back at the wagon Mason turned to Freeman and placed his hand on the man's shoulder. "I'm heading home. Stay as long as you want, but I suggest you think twice about going back over there. "

Freeman shoved his hand in his pocket and pulled out four silver dollars. Ned here found these along the front of the cave. Said he saw a few more on the inside but didn't go any farther when the bats came out."

"You think this is part of that shipment?"

"Positive," Freeman declared. He pointed at the date. "Like I told you before we had a larger print put on these coins so we could identify them in case something like this happened. I'd bet my life on it."

"And you will bet your life on it if you go inside that cave," Mason said.

Freeman shoved the coins back in his pocket. "That's what we need to consider. Is it worth the risk?"

"I'd say no, but that's up to you."

"That exactly what we're trying to decide."

He shook his head. "Well, good luck." He turned and lifted onto his horse, then rode away.

It was going on four o'clock when he arrived back at the stable. As he stepped from the saddle, he heard a ruckus. He glanced down as Kitty rushed across the toe of his boot with his collie hot on her trail. He smiled. *Never saw a dog and cat play like these two.* He shook his head as they rounded the corner and disappeared behind the building. He had to admit Dixie ran pretty fast for an old dog.

*Not quite sure what she'd do with that cat if she ever caught it. One thing for sure, with those claws, that cat would probably cure Dixie from ever chasing her again.* He chuckled beneath is breath as he slid the saddle from Midnight's back. After putting away his gear, he closed the latch on the tack room door and glanced up. His heart skipped a beat as Jenny entered the corridor, leading Ibn toward his stall.

"Hey," he said, stepping forward.

She peered over her shoulder and grinned. "Be right there," she said. A couple of minutes later, she returned and hung the lead rope on a nearby hook. "How did it go today? Did they find what they were looking for?"

"Yes and no," he replied leaning his shoulder against support post. "There was an unexpected delay in their progress.

"Delay," she repeated creasing a frown.

"Yes. I forgot to mention to Freeman that there was a cave near the falls. Hard telling how many bats live in there. Anyway, the workers must've got near the entrance and hundreds of those vicious creatures came swarming out. Mad as hell. We all ran for cover. The workers near the cave jumped in the river. It was quite a sight. They were screamin' and jumpin' like their pants were on fire. A couple of them nearly drown, just like you. When I left, they'd all got back safe and were discussing what they should do next."

"I know what I'd do," she stated, leaning against a feed barrel.

"And what would that be?" he asked, cocking a brow.

"I wouldn't go back. I hate those devils. I don't even like to come out to the barn at night because they are out chasing bugs. If one of those got caught in my hair, I'd die right on the spot."

He reared back laughing, then he turned and caught a glimpse of Freeman bringing the wagon to a stop in front of the stable door. Straightening, he proceeded outside. The men in back of the wagon gave a wave as he stepped up beside Freeman. "Hey, Sid. You stopping your search for the day?"

"Ya, I think we're done period," he stated, rubbing his thumb against the leather reins. "I'm so damn tired of chasing after that money. You'd think I'd be happy to finally find it, but no... something else to block the way. I can't ask these men to risk their lives, no matter how much money's in there. I say to hell with it. I truly believe it's there...but what if it isn't. No. I'm done. Let those treasure hunters find it."

"I understand," Mason said. "Don't think I'd chance it."

Jenny eased up alongside him. "So what're you going to do?" she asked Freeman. "Won't you get in trouble if you tell your commander you found the missing shipment, but refuse to bring it in. Isn't there a lot of gold and silver in there?"

"Probably, but I'll just tell them someone found it first and all that was left was a few loose coins near the sight. I'll tell them as far as I'm concerned the case is closed. My thought is, if someone finds, it they're welcome to it."

"Here, here," a voice shouted over Freeman's shoulder.

Mason raised an open palm. "Well, good luck, Sid. If you're

every back this way again, stop in to see us. You're always welcome."

Freeman gave his hand a brisk shake. "Thanks. I appreciate that." On a glance over his shoulder, he said, "Let's go home, men. It's been a long day."

They all waved goodbye as the wagon rattled off up the lane to the main road.

"He was sure a nice man," Jenny said.

"Smart, too," Mason chuckled as he shifted and looked down upon her beautiful features. "How about coming up to my place after dinner tonight? I'd like to taste those sweet lips of yours, again."

"I'd love to," she whispered, pressing close against his ribs.

"How about we say around eight?" he muttered, brushing his lips against her golden locks of hair.

Her eyes drifted shut. "Yes, I'll be there."

Her foreman cornered the build. He hesitated and cleared his throat. Jenny's eyes fluttered open and she stepped aside and looked away.

Mason felt the weight of her embarrassment and gave the man a nod, then looked at her and said, "I need to get to the office. We'll talk later."

"Yes, later," she said as her cheeks flushed with heat. Quickly, she retreated back into the barn.

Just before eight she entered Mason's office and called out his name.

"Lock the door and come on up," he said in a jovial tone.

She flipped the latch and made her way up the narrow staircase. Her feet had no more than covered the landing and he swept her up into his arms. "Wow," she swooned, wrapping her arms around his neck. "You certainly know how to take a woman's breath away." Her eyes met his. Doesn't this hurt your shoulder?"

"My dear Jenny, you are worth the pain," he teased. "Besides, I took a pain pill. It'll probably hurt later, but not right now." He swirled her around a couple of times more and each rotation took them closer to the bed.

"You're making me dizzy," she said, lowering her eyelids.

At that moment, he kissed her, deep and passionate, as if reaching for her soul.

"Mmm," she moaned. "That was wonderful," she whispered. "Don't stop."

"I don't intend to," he said, placing her on the bed. His heart thundered against his chest as he lowered beside her. "I've been thinking about you all day." He buried his face in her golden tresses and inhaled her scent. The sweet fragrance of lilac filled his nostrils and he released a soothing sigh of delight. Without remorse, he burned a trail of kisses down her neck and across the arch to her shoulder. A soft growl rumbled from deep within his throat. Gently, he untied the ribbon that held together the front of her dress. His lips found hers as his hand slipped beneath the cloth and covered her young breast. He caressed the tender flesh, then a moment later he turned away and stood. "Come, let me undress you," he said, holding out his hand.

She grasped his moist palm and pulled to her feet. Stepping from her dress she bumped the night table. The lantern flickered. Quickly, she turned and settled the piece, then began to lower the wick.

"Don't turn it off," he said. "I want to see you. Every inch of your gorgeous body. You fascinate me and I want to enjoy every moment with you."

She lowered her gaze, then removed her garments.

"Beautiful," he said, his breath heavy with passion. "This will be a night to remember."

# Chapter Twenty-eight

Mason rolled to the bedside and sat up. Stretching, he yawned, then coughed a couple of time. Each morning his cough seemed a little worse. *Must be catching a cold. That's about all winters are good for.* He raked his fingers through his hair, then glanced at the window. *Snowing. Another sign winter is upon us, but I guess it's time; today's the first of November.*

On a sigh and another cough, he leveled his feet on the cool floor and trekked to the window. Pushing the curtain aside, a full view of the snow-covered hillside came into view. Large flakes floated down like a goose feather painting a masterpiece across the landscape. A grin tugged at his lips. *Have to admit, it is beautiful.*

He glanced at the clock. Quarter after eight. Guess there'll be no work on the shop today. Now they had the frame up, he was anxious to get it finished. It was sure a blessing to have Pack home to help with the construction. He's always been one to jump in and help on most every project. *I could not have asked for a better friend.*

His thoughts were suddenly interrupted by another round of coughing. "Damn," he jeered aloud. "Enough of that." Concern creased his forehead and he stepped over and spit in the chamber pot. Instantly a red smear of blood floated to the surface. "Wow, this is more serious than I thought," he mumbled. He wiped his lips on the hand towel and proceeded to get dressed.

Twenty minutes later, he trudged through the snow on his way to the stable. A dark cloud, heavy with moisture lurked overhead. He lifted his collar against the driving wind. If it weren't for a need to feed Midnight, he sure as hell wouldn't be out in this miserable storm. He stepped inside and slid the door shut. As he stomped his feet, kicking off the snow, Jenny appeared in the corridor.

"I thought I heard somebody," she said. "Were you surprised at the snow?"

"Not really," he said removing his gloves. "It's that time of year."

"I bet we've got at least three inches on the ground. Wonder how much more we'll get?"

Mason lifted the lid on the grain barrel and took out a scoop. "Hard to tell. Maybe an inch or two more."

She followed him as he went to Midnight's stall and dumped the grain in the feed box. "I didn't know you got that much snow in this part of the country," she said, her words slipping across his shoulder.

"Sometimes," he said in an uninterested tone. He pushed past her and gathered a portion of an open bale of hay and shoved it in the rack for the horse to feed on.

"Is there something wrong?" she asked, placing her gloved hands atop her hips.

He stopped and stared at her. "Sorry. I don't feel well today. Think I'm catching a cold."

Maybe we fanned the covers too much last night," she said with a smirk.

He gave her a cold and uncaring glare.

Her expression turned solemn and she glanced away.

"Where is everyone?" he asked as he once again pushed past her.

"They haven't shown up yet," she said, her voice meek and filled with hurt.

"Don't they know the horses need care no matter if there's snow or not?" he grumbled. He gathered a bucket of water from the well and filled Midnight's barrel. Locking the stall gate, he looked at her for a long moment. "Do you need my help?" he asked. "If not, I'm going back to my office."

"No," she replied without showing her true emotion. "I can handle things here. You go right on. While you're there, drink another cup of hot coffee. It'll help, if you have a sore throat."

Giving a nod, he started to step forward when Kitty came bounding around the corner with Dixie hot on her trail. As soon as the cat passed, he lifted his foot, then grabbed the collie by the nap of her neck. "Stop it, Dixie," he shouted. "Leave that cat alone." He grasped a lead hanging on a nearby hook and tied the end around the dog's neck. "In fact, you come with me. Let that cat have a little peace for once."

The dog wagged her tail, then looked at kitty and barked as if to say we'll play later.

Jenny smiled as the two walked out the door into the falling snow. "What a grouch," she said beneath her breath. In her mind's eye, she was not sure this was the same man that sent her world spinning just hours ago. She drew a deep breath. *I know he feels badly, but what a difference. Oh well, I guess we all have days we don't feel up to par. No matter, I love him anyway. When I'm in his arms the rest of the world disappears. I love him so much.*

Mason slammed the front door of his office and flipped the lock closed. Bending, he released the rope from the dog's neck and pitched it onto a nearby bench. With a huff, he removed his coat, then made his way to the kitchen. Deep in thought, he fixed himself a cup of coffee as Jenny had suggested. His throat wasn't sore, but he felt chilled from being out in the cold. Moments later, with the steaming brew in hand, he stepped back into the office. His eyes narrowed as he glanced around the room. With the weather so bad, there would be no business, that was for damn sure. His throat tickled and he sputtered a ragged cough. Concern filled his thoughts once more. *Think I'll go back to bed for a while; maybe I'll feel better if I take a nap.*

Two steps up the stairs and Dixie jumped up to follow. "No," he said. "You stay."

The dog hunkered down and return to the door mat.

Jenny assembled the workers after morning chores. "There's no need for you men to stay in this inclement weather," she announced. "Outdoor activity, such as workouts and exercise, is out of the question. I want to thank you all for coming in on such a miserable day. I'm proud of you for being so dedicated. I'll take care of the evening chores, so go home. Stay safe and warm and enjoy being with your families."

"Thanks, Miss Jones," her foreman said, giving her a guarded hug. "See you tomorrow,"

The men echoed his words as they stepped past her and followed him out the door.

The huge barn door rolled shut and she glanced out through a nearby window. As the men rode past, she focused on the office across the way. There was no sign of Mason or his dog. Concern for his health swept in. *Perhaps he was sicker than she thought. Surely he would have shown signs of something before now.* She needed to check on him on her way home.

Bright light reflected a stinging glare off the snow drifts on the lane and she glanced up. She squinted as the sun broke through the clouds. "Good," she said aloud. *I think I'll just stay here for a while and let some of the snow melt before I go up to the house.* She exhaled on a snicker. *I'd probably take a nap anyway. I can make good use of that time if I stay here and straighten up the tack room.*

After a good hour and a half of thorough cleaning, she closed the tack room door. A quick glance out the window revealed spotty patches of grass on the hillside and water dripping from the icicles that dangled from above the window. Her gaze cut to the office across the lane. There was still no sign of Mason. She released a puff of displeasure, then strode up the corridor. Nearing the end stalls she was taken back by a creak from the roller on the stable door. Wide eyed, she swung around.

The man in black stepped into view.

Jenny swallowed hard as her heart slammed against her ribs. "You," she said, her tone filled with loathing.

A villainous smiled creased his lips. He slowly pulled off his gloves and removed his hat, then pitched them aside. "Where's your friend?" he growled.

Her mind whirled, searching for a reply. "He's here. He-he'll be right back."

The man eased forward. His dark eyes snapped with an evil glare and his black stringy hair lay close to his head. This was the first time she'd ever seen this villain up close. His rotten stained teeth could hardly be seen beneath a ragged mustache. She swallowed hard as he drew nearer. Her fear heightened and she scanned the corridor for protection. What was this monster going to do? A pitchfork stood against a nearby stall door, but out of her reach. Her only hope for escape was to bolt past him. Corralling her fear, she raised her chin. "What is it you want?"

A vicious laugh followed. "For the moment, I'll settle for you, sweetie. It's been a while since I've had a clean woman. You'll do just fine."

"No," she said, stiffening her position. "Get out of here or I'll.."

"You'll what, precious? Call for help?" He laughed again. "The horses can't help you. I think you're mine for the taking."

She backed up a step.

"Ah, don't be afraid. I won't hurt you. Not if you co-operate. I like my women clean and soft. If you're good, I'll be good to you. You may even enjoy it."

"Go away, you slime ball. I'll never let you touch me," she sneered.

He lunged forward and she darted to the side. As he stumbled, she tried to make her escape, but he was too quick. His calloused hand reached out and grabbed her arm.

She gasped.

He shoved her against the stall.

On a wicked scream, she pounded her fist against the side of his head.

His free hand grabbed her wrist and he slammed his six-foot frame against her, pinning her against the wood.

She fought to catch her breath as his mouth lowered onto her neck. She screamed again.

Immediately, he released her arm and slammed his sweaty palm across her mouth. "Shut up, bitch. You're going to be mine, like it or not," he snarled. "You may as well like it, because this will be the last thing you do before I kill you and pretty boy."

The taste of his grimy hand against her mouth made her stomach churn. Tears rolled down her cheeks. How could she escape this monster? He pressed her so tight against the wood, she struggled to catch her breath. "Please," she pleaded. "Don't do this."

"Oh, but you'll like it," he said as he thrashed against her trying to unbutton his pants.

She closed her eyes and wept out loud.

"Well, well, well, what do we have here," Mason's voice echoed in her ears. He grabbed the man by the back of his neck and shoved him to the ground.

Jenny leaped sideways and hid behind her hero. "Oh, God, Mason, I'm so glad you're here."

He stepped forward and towered over the man. "What the hell you think you're doing?" he asked.

The treasure hunter lifted onto his elbow, but said nothing.

"Get up, you sonofabitch," Mason ordered.

"He-he came to kill us," Jenny rasped, still fighting for each breath.

Mason coughed, then snickered. "He's not going to kill us. He wants the money and, beings I know where it is, he won't kill us; he'd rather be rich." He lowered into the man's ruddy face. "Right?"

The man lifted and staggered to his feet.

"That piece of map you have isn't worth a damn," Mason said. "You were right. The money is near here, but not on my property. So, you can kill us or I can tell you where it is and you get the hell out of our lives. It's your choice. What'll it be?"

The treasure hunter straightened and nodded. "Tell me where it is and I'll never bother you again."

Mason turned to Jenny. "Is that agreeable with you?"

"Yes, just make him go away," she said, her hand clamped tight on his arm.

"All right." His glare cut to the man in black. "Take the lane back to the falls. There's a log raft tied nearby. Take it across the water. You'll find a cave hidden behind heavy underbrush. The money is hidden about twenty-five feet back into the cave. You'll see a few coins scattered inside, but the real treasure is hidden farther in. In fact, I'll even give you this," he said, handing the man a lantern. "You may need it. It's dark in there. I wouldn't want you to get lost."

The man gathered his hat and gloves and lumbered to the door, then turned to face them. "Thanks," he mumbled and exited.

"Why did you tell him?" she asked, her eyes filled with questions.

He smiled. "You'll find out. He deserves every dollar he can find." He cleared his throat. "I need to go back to bed."

She jerked on his arm. "How did you know he was here?"

"I passed the window and saw his horse tied out front. You really should lock that door when you're here alone."

Jenny watched his shoulder droop as he sauntered back home. "I just don't have a good feeling about everything that has happened today. Perhaps tomorrow will be better," she spoke aloud.

She glanced down and saw Kitty sitting by her food bowl. Smiling, she scooped up the cat. "Let's go see what Danny is doing, want too?" One quick glance around and all was secure. She released her anxiety on a sigh and left the building.

# Chapter Twenty-nine

Moonlight cast eerie shadows across the ceiling and walls. Mason stared into the darkness, begging for morning's light to appear. He tossed among the covers until he finally sat up and grabbed his robe from the end of the bed. On a huff, he glanced at the clock. Three-ten. *Damn, I shouldn't have slept so much yesterday. I knew this would happen.* He rolled out of bed and shoved his arms into the cotton robe, then jammed his feet into his slippers and headed down to the kitchen.

After fixing a hot cup of coffee, he scooped up a biscuit he'd brought home from supper at Jenny's two nights before. As he lowered onto the chair at the table, he began to cough. Once the coughing fit ended, he pulled the handkerchief from his pocket and wiped his lips. Upon folding the cloth, he noticed a few spots of red. His gaze deepened. "Blood," he whispered. *Damn it, anyway. I need to find out what's going on. I know I probably have a fever because I feel chilled. Think I'll go to the doctor and get checked out. Maybe I need some medicine to get over this.*

He took a big gulp of his brew and closed his eyes. Thoughts of Jenny rushed into his mind. Her beauty was as pure as gold.

A smiled tugged at his mouth. *I wish I had the money. I'd give her everything her heart desired. She's all I think about. Maybe that's what it's like to be in love.*

At seven a.m. he locked the office door and went to the stable. Yesterday's snow only remained in patches along the grassy hillside. He kicked the mud from his boots upon entering the building and glanced up at the sound of clanging feed buckets. A couple of the workers, had arrived and were beginning their morning chores. Mason gave them a nod as they passed by, then he saddled Midnight and headed for town.

A little before noon, he returned and rode straight to Pack's house. He reined the horse to a stop and sat silent for a moment, deep in thought. He must tell his friend the truth. Things were going to be different and he wanted to make sure Pack could handle the pressure.

Several minutes later, he ease from the saddle and trudged up the steps to the front entrance. Pulling a deep breath, he rapped his knuckles on the oak door, then stepped back.

Pack soon came to the door, completely dressed, but nothing on his feet. Surprise swept across his dark features. "Don't tell me you wanta work today. Man, it's damn cold out there. Get on in here."

"I can't. Get you boots and a coat on. I need to talk to you."

The man's brows lowered. "What the hell's wrong with you? Get your ass in here."

"Do as I say, Pack. This is serious."

Confusion changed his expression and he backed into the entrance way and did as his friend asked. Seconds later, he appeared while he finished buttoning the wool coat. "This better be good," he mumbled, stepping out onto the porch.

"Don't get any closer," Mason said, holding his arm at full length between them. "I'm sick, Pack, and I need your help."

The man's dark eyes narrowed as he deepened his stare. "What's wrong?"

"The doctor isn't sure yet. He needs to do some tests, but he thinks I may have the Tuberculosis disease."

"TB?" he repeated, his tone pitching higher. "What the… How'd that happen?"

"I have no idea, but I want you not to tell anyone, especially Jenny. I'm going to tell her I have to go to Colorado to help my step-father. I'll tell her he's had a stroke and I must go run the ranch for him. I don't want her to know. That way, she won't question my being gone for a long time. In fact, I may never be able to come back. She needs to find someone who will love and care for her."

"Damn, Mason, what about the shop?"

"I want you to finish it just in case I can return one day. I'll give you the keys to my office and you run your business out of there. Just leave my shop closed for me so if and when I return…" He pulled the back of his collar up to detour the brisk north wind. "Will you do this for me?"

"Sure. You know I will," Pack said, with tears glistening in his eyes. "I love you, pal. Don't you dare go and die on me, you hear?"

"I'll sure as hell try not to," Mason said, tearing up as well.

"When you going to go?" Pack asked as his friend turned to leave.

Mason lifted into the saddle. "Probably in a day or so. I have to go to Chicago for more tests. I'll send you a wire and let you know the results."

"Good luck. You'll be in my prayers, my friend" Pack said, his voice cracking as he went back inside and closed the door.

Before Mason could get to the stable, the sheriff came galloping down the lane toward him. The man pulled up alongside him and asked, "You heading out?"

"No," Mason replied. "Going up to the house to see Jenny. "What you need?"

"Wanted you to know I haven't seen hide nor hair of that man you said threatened you. He must've left town. Bad thing is his brother's body is still at the funeral home waiting to be claimed."

"Well, he was here yesterday. Last I saw him, he was on his way back to the falls. He's still looking for that money he thinks is here on my land. There was another man here a few days earlier looking, too, but he gave up. Said it was too dangerous."

"Dangerous? How's that?" the sheriff asked, turning away from the wind in his face.

"People keep getting hurt. Maybe there's a curse on it. Myself, I think they're all crazy. If there was money hidden here, I'd a heard about it years ago. No one in my family mentioned it."

"Hmm, so what did the treasure-hunting guy say when he came back by?"

Mason snickered. "He never returned. May still be back there looking."

"Mind if I ride back and take a look?"

"Not at all. I should be back in my office when you return. Let me know if you find him. I've been wondering myself. I've got a bad cold or I'd go with you. Just be careful. A lot of bad things happening back there."

The sheriff nodded, then rode off.

Chilled to the bone, Mason guided Midnight over to his office and went inside. He removed his coat, hat and glove, then strode to the kitchen and put a pot of coffee on the stove. As the brew warmed, he paced the floor, wondering how he was going to tell Jenny such a lie and make it believable. He cared so much about her and didn't want to hurt her, but it would be the best thing for her in the long run.

Steam rose from the pot and he stepped over and poured the hot brew into the porcelain cup and took a sip. Damn that tasted good. He wrapped his hands tight around the warmth and walked back into his office and lowered onto the desk chair. He took another drink, then placed the coffee on his desk and leaned back. His eyes drifted shut and instantly an image of her appeared. He envisioned her flawless naked body in his arms and how smooth her skin felt as he lowered his hands and cups her hips in his palms. He would carry such beautiful memories for the rest of his life.

His eyes eased open and he coughed, then took another drink of coffee. How could he live, knowing he turned his back on her and walked away. The thought of her being with another man cut through his soul like a jagged knife. A tear eased out and rolled down his cheek.

He shook his head. Why did this have to happen? Why couldn't he live like his parents and have years of love and companionship? "Damn it," he raged, "I don't want to be sick." He grabbed the cup and downed the last of the brew, then surged to his feet. "I need to get this done now," he shouted as he grabbed his coat and gloves and dashed out the door.

Minutes later, he saw her buggy at the stable. On a heavy groan he stepped into the building and called her name. Moments seemed like hours as he waited for her response.

"Yes," she said, appearing in the doorway of the tack room. "I'll be right there."

He glanced around. The scrape of shovels cleaning in a nearby stall made his muscles tighten. What he had to say had to be in private. He swung around and held his hand out. "Stop," he ordered. "I need you to go back inside. I have to talk to you alone. You're not going to like what I say."

Stunned, she glared at him for a moment, then stepped back inside the tack room. "What is it?" she asked as he shut the door behind him.

"I think you'd better sit down."

Puzzled, she strode over and eased down onto a small wooden

barrel. "What's wrong, Mason? Are you feeling worse?"

"No, I got a telegram that my stepfather has had a stroke and I need to leave for Colorado right away. I may be gone a long time and I want you to know I care about you, but I won't be able to see you anymore."

"What?" she said, her voice pitched higher. She stared at him, stunned, as she fought to understand. Her gaze appeared to be like a light that stunned her comprehension. Finally, she blinked and asked, "What about your business and your shop?"

"Pack will take care of all that. I may be gone a year. It may be five years. I don't know. But, I have to go. I want you to know I've enjoyed our time together, but you need to find someone who will love you and take care of you."

"I don't need anyone else. It's you I care about." Tears ran down her cheeks. "I love you. I will always love you. Don't you know that?" She leaned forward and cried out loud.

"I'm sorry," he said. "I don't want to hurt you, but this is something I must do. I owe him this. He helped me start my business. You are a lovely person. You'll find someone else."

"I don't want anyone else. I have the one I want. Please take me with you. I'll sell my place. We don't have to get married. I'll even help you with chores on the ranch."

"No, Jenny. I can't take you away from here. This is your home now." He walked to the door. "Who knows what the future will bring? Take care of yourself. If ever I can, I'll be back, but for now I have to say goodbye."

He rushed out of the building, his heart pumping a million miles a minute. Relief in telling her was overrun by guilt in lying to her. How could he live with himself knowing how he'd broken her heart? He forced back tears as he slammed the office door shut and flopped onto his chair at the desk. What a nightmare. There was no pride in hurting her, but he could not be with her and take a chance of her catching this disease.

In a daze he sat at his desk staring at the window. *So much has happened this year, my mind is whirling. I feel like ten years have been rolled into one. I don't know if I can stand being in a hospital for God only knows how long. My only hope is that the doctor is wrong and this is nothing more than a common cold instead of such a horrible disease. I don't think I can stand living anywhere but here in Kentucky.*

Tears blurred his vision and he lowered his head. *God help me. I can't do this alone.*

# Chapter Thirty

A heavy knock on the office door brought Mason forward in his chair. On a frown, he rose, then traversed the room and opened the door.

The sheriff stepped inside. "Damn, it's cold out there," he said, pulling off his glove and blowing into his fist. His nose and cheeks were as red as a bowl of cherries.

"Yes, it's that north wind. The holidays will be here before you know it, "Mason said. He peeked over the man's shoulder as he closed the door. "Is that the treasure hunter you have across the saddle of his horse?"

"Sure is," he replied. "He must've drowned. I found him washed up on the bank near the place where you said the girl's grandfather got shot. The fella had marks all over his face and in his hair. Don't know what happened to him, but he was a goner for sure."

Sounds like he may have gone in that cave on the other side of the falls. From what I hear, it's full of bats."

"Could've been. Whatever it was, got him good. Anyway, I'm taking him back and leavin' him with that brother of his that died.

If'n no one claims them, we'll just put 'em in the city cemetery with a few other unclaimed bodies." Sheriff shook his head. "It's amazing how nobody wants 'em after their dead."

Maybe they don't have any family to claim 'em. Might be that's why they choose that kinda life."

"No matter, 'least he'll be no more trouble. You can get a good night's sleep without worrying about him showin' up again." He shoved his hands back in his gloves and grasped the door knob, then he faced Mason once more. "Do you really think there's a treasure back there?"

Mason chuckled. "Maybe...maybe not. Myself...I doubt it, but who knows. Others sure believe it."

"Ya, well, I doubt it, too. Guess some folks just need a dream to give them hope for a better life. Me, I'm just glad to be alive." He grinned, then opened the door and stopped midway. "Oh, one last thing. I saw the circuit judge and he overruled the county judge in Brad's favor. "Said he'd let Brad go after two years if'n he behaved."

"That's great news. Thanks for letting me know. "

"You bet," he said, then gave a nod. "Have a good day."

Mason ate an early dinner that evening, then packed his clothes and went to bed. A million thoughts tumbled through his head. There were things he needed to tell Pack, things he must remember to do before he leaves, but most of all, he thought of Jenny. Memories of their times together, the love they shared, and, yes, the expression on her face when he said he could no longer see her. She was devastated and he knew it. He'd expected her to cling to him and beg him not to go, but she held her composure. God, how he wanted to take her in his armS and tell her it wasn't true.

After three hours of misery, he tossed the covers aside and trekked across the room. His hand trembled as he opened the medicine bottle and downed the last pain pill. Surely this would allow him to have a decent night's sleep. Starting back to bed, another coughing fit stopped him in his tracks and he bent over, coughing until he heaved. Once he caught his breath, he straightened, then rushed over and collapsed on the mattress. He grabbed the covers and pulled them over his head, mumbling a curse as he squeezed his eyes tight. He must get this cured. No way could he stand a lifetime fighting this disease.

It was five a.m. when Mason rolled out of bed. He dragged his fingers through his hair and staggered over to the window. "Mmm, another dreary day," he mumbled. "Looks the way I feel."

He washed up, then dressed and went downstairs to finish storing things away. Damn, how he hated to leave. His whole world revolved around this place. He missed it already and he hadn't even left yet. Pushing his depression aside, he put on his coat and took a brisk walk to Pack's house. A sharp knock on the wooden panel brought his friend to the door.

"Come on in," he said, stepping aside for Mason to enter. "How about a cup of coffee to warm your innards?"

"Sure," he replied and strode over to the fireplace and propped his foot up on the hearth. He fought to catch his breath as he held his hands toward the burning logs. "I shouldn't be in here, you know." Pack held out the cup of brew and Mason glared at it. "On second thought, I'd better not drink from your cup. Thanks, anyway."

Pack lowered the mug onto a nearby table. "You're having a tough time, aren't you?"

Mason nodded. "I'm miserable," he admitted. "I'll get my sayin' done and get out of here. I have a couple of things I want you to do for me."

"Sure," Pack replied, his features filled with concern.

"First of all, tell Jenny she won't be bothered by the treasure hunter anymore. " On short, choppy breaths he explained what the sheriff told him.

"Folks has sure made a big fuss about that money," Pack said, taking a sip of his coffee. "Maybe now they'll leave us alone. Like you said, maybe that's just a tale handed down from one generation to another. Probably made up by some fool back during the war."

"Yes, I agree. Anyway, the next thing I want you to do is complete the shop and get it up and running again. Use my office as much as you want." He shoved his hand into his pocket and pulled out the key, then handed it to Pack. "I left money in the safe. Use as much of it as you need. You know the combination. I don't have much, but use what you need."

"I-I appreciate that," Pack stammered as he stared at the piece of metal in his palm.

"Lastly, I need you to get the vet out here next week and have Midnight gelded. I don't want him giving Jenny anymore grief when she breeds Ibn. Besides, I want the boy to have my horse. Danny needs his own horse and Midnight will be a perfect companion for him." He lowered his foot from the hearth and straightened. "Also, tell Jenny that the boy's father had his sentence reduced and should be home in a couple of years. I'm sure he will be anxious to see him."

Mason's eyes widened and he wrenched. "Ugh, I'm about to cough. I've got to get out of here." His eyes blurred as he stared at his friend. "Good luck, Pack. I'll miss you. Damnit, I hope I see you again one day." He patted Pack's shoulder and rushed out the door.

Twenty-four hours later, Mason arrived in Chicago, Illinois, and went directly to the medical center to visit Dr. West. The specialist was one of the best in treating tuberculosis.

Mason's hands trembled and his heart drummed against his chest as he strode into the examination room. Moments later, a white haired man wearing dark rimmed glasses appeared in the doorway. He wore a white coat over his street clothes and carried a yellow folder in his hand. "Mason Jackson," the man said, peering over his glasses.

"Yes," he replied, swallowing hard.

"Have a seat. I need for you to tell me about what you do and the symptoms you have been experiencing, then I need to examine you. That should give me some idea about whether you have TB or something else is going on."

Mason nodded, then proceeded to tell the doctor everything.

A little over an hour later and after a thorough examination the doctor stated, "Your symptoms are mild. I'm not certain you have tuberculosis. I do need you to isolate yourself for six months, then come back and we'll see how you are." He scribbled down a few notes on his chart, then handed Mason the sheet of paper. "Here is what I want you to do and beneath that are things you should watch for. If you get worse, by all means come back immediately. Do you have somewhere you can go and not expose yourself to the public?"

"Yes. My step-father has a ranch in Colorado. There's a cabin on his property up in the foothills he uses when he goes hunting. I'm sure I can stay there. He can bring me food and supplies every week or so."

"Good. Be sure to have him cover his nose and mouth with a bandana or something when he comes to see you."

Mason nodded. "I'll notify him right away that I'm coming."

"Good luck son," the doc said, walking him to the door. "I hope this is nothing more than a bad infection. If you do as I ask, I think you'll be fine. Make an appointment at the desk out front for six months from now. I'll see you then."

"All right. Thank you, Dr. West."

The man nodded, then said, "Uh, the nurse will give you a mask to wear until you reach your destination. Be sure to use it."

"Yes, sir," he said, and the doctor disappeared into an adjoining room.

Six months drug by like six years. There were days Mason

missed home so much he felt sick to his stomach. He tried to keep his mind busy by whittling on sticks he found around the cabin. In a few weeks' time, he'd carved a complete chess set. After that, he began carving little animal figures to give to Danny if and when he ever returned home.

The days went by at a snail's pace. Some days, it snowed all day and he never got out of the cabin. Other days, the wind blew like a banshee. He often wondered if spring would ever arrive.

The mornings he could get to the nearby stream, he saw his reflection in the clear mountain water. His hair and beard had grown to a point where he hardly recognized himself; revealing the true weight of his isolation. Not to his liking, he'd become a real mountain man.

In the meantime, Jenny was spending most of her time in her bedroom staring out the window.

There were days her eyes were so swollen from crying she would not go down for dinner. Her life had been ripped apart and she sobbed constantly. Every moment of ever day her thoughts were of Mason. She recalled him telling her that he could no longer be with her. The words cut through her heart like a dagger. How could he do this to her? She loved him so much.

Even her love for the horses vanished. She no longer went to the stable. One by one, she sold off the beautiful Arabians and dismissed all of her workers, except her foreman. Life was just not worth living without the man she loved.

Mason's six months of solitude ended on the fifth of May.

He gathered his thing and asked his step father to ship home his collection of novelty items that he'd carved for Danny. That was, if the doctor released him. If not, he'd be back for God knows how long next time.

Mason stepped on the train; clean shaven and wearing clean clothes. He lifted his chin with confidence that the future would be brighter. Smiling, he pulled a deep breath. His lungs didn't hurt and he no longer coughed. In fact, he felt as strong as the day he met Jenny. His lips widened. *Jenny. My beautiful, precious Jenny. I can't wait to see her again. I need to make up for the hurt I caused her. That is, unless she's found someone new.*

"All aboard," the conductor shouted.

"By all means," he chuckled. "Let's get going."

# Chapter Thirty-one

Kentucky bluegrass moved in the fields like an ocean wave, rolling in rhythm with each gust of wind. The blue sky above, adorned with white wispy clouds, painted a beautiful backdrop to welcome Mason home. Even the birds in nearby trees chattered in excitement, announcing his arrival. He glanced up and smiled. *It feels good to be going home.*

He turned the rented buggy into the lane to what was once the Jackson Estate. He reined the horse to a stop at the top of the hill and skimmed his gaze over the land. A chill rippled beneath his skin. *This is my world. The land where I belong.* His gaze blurred as so many memories tumbled through his mind.

Moments later, he clucked the horse forward and drove to his office. Excitement swept over him as he jumped from the buggy and rushed in the door.

Pack looked up from his paper work, then came to his feet. A moment later, they greeted each other with an endearing hug and stepped back.

"Damn, it's good to see you," Mason said, then glanced around the room. "Everything looks just like I left it."

"Sorry I couldn't pick you up at the station," Pack said as he turned and gathered the invoices on the desk. "I had a client picking up an order at noon. He was here from Louisville. I couldn't tell him not to come."

"No problem. I rented a buggy at the stable in town." He gestured his thumb over his right shoulder. "They did a nice job building the new shop."

"Yes. I opened up a couple of weeks ago" Pack said, slipping the papers into the top drawer.

"What about Jenny? Is she all right?"

Pack shook his head. "She hasn't been herself since you left. She sold off all her horses and rarely comes to the stable."

"Is she seeing anyone?"

"Lord, no. I see her out taking walks with Danny, but that's about all."

Mason strode over and stared out the window. "Is she up at the house now?"

"Don't think so. She, Agnes and the boy left early this morning. Think they went shopping for the boy some new clothes. He's outgrowin' everything he has."

"What about you? Everything all right with you?"

"Sure. I guess you don't know I married Rose 'bout a month ago. She's over at the house now washin' clothes. In fact, we're going to have a baby come winter."

"Well, you ole dog. I'm happy for you."

"What about you? Did the doctor say you're gonna be all

right?"

"He seems to think so. He didn't see any signs of the disease, but to be on the safe side, I have to go back in a year to see him."

Pack stepped to the door. "Come on, let go next door and I'll show you the inside of our new shop."

"That's great, I'd like that."

Pack opened the door and just as he was about to step forward, Kitty came running in between his legs. An instant later, Dixie rushed in behind her, growling. The cat jumped up on the shelf and knocked over Kathryn's picture, then pushed in to hide behind the bird cage. The metal piece rocked and teetered on the edge of the shelf.

"No," Mason yelled and grabbed at the dog.

Pack slammed the door shut and ran to catch the cage. As he approached, he stumbled and fell to his knees.

Frightened, Kitty jumped to the floor and the cage came crashing down.

The bottom of the cage came apart and scattered broken pieces across the floor.

"Damn it, cat," Mason shouted as Kitty ran beneath the desk.

Dixie lunged forward to attack, but instead knocked the broken cage up against the wall.

"What can I do?" Pack asked, staggering to his feet.

"Here, take Dixie and put her outside. Just leave the cat. She's scared. She'll be all right where she is for now."

Pack took the dog and Mason leaned forward and picked

up the broken cage. "Damnit," he said, then reached over and straightened his mother's picture. "I'm so sorry. I'll get it fixed. It'll be like new," he said, speaking to her image in the frame. Frustration built as he scanned the scattered pieces. A moment later, he noticed something sticking out from between the two pieces of metal that made up the bottom. He lowered on one knee and slowly pulled it out. A frown tugged at his brow. His breath caught as he spread the paper open.

His friend walked up beside him. "What's that?" he asked.

Mason glanced up. "It's a letter to my mother."

"Your mother?"

Pack lowered next to him and pinched his eyes tight to get a better look. "What does it say?"

"It says, 'Dearest Kathryn, when you find this I will be in a better place. As you already know I left you my property, but I neglected to tell you I have one last treat to show you how much I appreciated all that you did for me. Years ago, during the war, I was out coon hunting one night back near the falls. I heard voices so I hunkered down and listened. There were Union soldiers carrying a load of silver and gold across country. Their scout had spotted Rebs up ahead, so they decided to hide the shipment among the rocks below the falls.'"

"Then there really was a treasure back there," Pack said, straightening.

Mason stared at him, not believing what he'd just read.

"Well, go on, read the rest," Pack insisted, punching on his back with his fingertips.

"All right, all right. He says, 'I watched them draw up a map and split it among them. They agreed to come back in a year and meet at the falls to split the money. Before they could leave, the bats came from the cave and attack them and they ran away. The next day, I returned and gathered the money.

But before I left, I took a hand full of coins and threw in the cave so anyone searching for it would think it was there. I brought the coins home and buried them in a beer keg beneath the golden raintree you loved so much. With all my love, I leave this to you. I want you and your family to enjoy this treasure forever more. Your loving friend and neighbor, J. Watson.'"

"Well, I'll be damned. There really is something to those stories." Mason said, staring at the paper. "And all the while the truth was sitting here on the shelf right beside me."

"So, what're you going to do now," Pack asked, scratching his head. "I don't remember any golden raintrees around here."

"Mother spoke of that tree often. It was back along the tree line by the woods. It stood about fifty paces off the road to the falls. The tornado that crossed our land several years ago tore it down. There's nothing left of it but the stump."

"Wow, you're rich," Pack said, bubbling with excitement.

After a long moment, Mason folded the letter and shoved it in his pocket, then gathered the broken pieces and placed them on the shelf.

"So, what are you gonna do?" his friend asked.

Mason's dazed stare met Pack's. "I guess we need to see if it's true."

"You're damn right, we should. I'll go get the shovels. There's a couple in the barn we can use."

"Not so fast. I need to bring in my travel bags and put away the horse and buggy."

"All right, you do that and I'll get the wagon ready," he said, his voice filled with eagerness. "Damn, what a great day. You came home and then found out you're rich and in the same day."

Mason laughed, "Well, I'm not rich yet. Let's find those kegs first, then we can celebrate."

Seven hours later, Mason washed up and put on his best clothes, then scooped up the beautiful wild flower he'd picked earlier. His heart thundered with excitement as he trekked up the secret path to Jenny house. Thoughts mixed with doubts whirled in his head as he made his way to her front porch.

Would she be angry with him or would she accept his apology. Only time would tell and that time could be only minutes away.

Finally, he faced the front door. His mouth went dry as he raised his hand and twisted the bell. Agnes's husband answered the bell and offered a smile, then stepped aside. "I'll get her for you," he said as Mason entered the foyer and closed the door.

The flowers jittered in his hand as he awaited her arrival. A heartbeat later, she appeared in the parlor and faced him. "Jenny," he said, his voice meek and full of emotion.

She stepped forward; stopping an arm's length away. "I didn't know you were back," she muttered. "Is your stepfather well?"

"Yes, he's fine." He glanced down to steady his composure. "I want to apologize. I never meant to hurt you. I'd like to see you again if you will forgive me."

Tears began to stream down her cheeks. "I loved you so much. How could you do that to me?" She turned away. "I would've followed you to the ends of the earth."

He stepped up behind her and eased his hand onto her shoulder. "I love you, Jenny," he said, bringing her around to face him once more. "Please take these," he said, holding out the bouquet. "I want you to know I'm sorry and I'll never hurt you again."

She grasped the flowers, then threw her arms around his neck. "Oh, Mason, I missed you so much."

His lips met hers in a long and passionate kiss, then he pulled back, "Does that mean you forgive me?"

"Yes, yes. Just say you'll never leave me again."

He smiled. "I promise."

She gave him a kiss on the cheek, then grasped his hand and stepped toward the parlor.

His grip tightened and he pulled her to a stop. "Put the flower on the side table," he said and dipped his hand into his pocket.

Her features became solemn and her eyes filled with question. "What's wrong?"

"Hold out your hand," he ordered. "And close your eyes."

She lowered her brow, then did as he asked. Her features lightened as she responded to the cool round metal dropping into her palm.

"These are for you," he said as she opened her eyes and glazed upon six gold coins resting in her hand.

"Where did you…Are these from the treasure everyone's been searching for?"

He smiled and nodded. "I'll explain it all to you later. Right now, I want to ask you to marry me."

"Oh, yes, Mason, of course I will," she said, "but I'd marry you if you were poor. The money doesn't matter."

"I plan to make you the happiest woman in the world. You can shop, travel and do whatever your heart desires."

"My heart only desires to be with you, my darling. Life with you is all I want." She kissed him, then said, "Come, I can't wait to tell everyone the good news."

That night, he took her home with him and they sealed their promise to each other. The following weekend they were united in marriage with Pack and Rose as their witnesses. The two young lovers would continue to thrive on the beautiful estate near Lexington, Kentucky. Mason, as a talented craftsman, and Jenny at his side. Good fortune had smiled upon the Jackson family once more.

# About the Author

    I hope you've enjoyed reading **WHISPERS OF THE HEART**, book FOUR in the four-book series "The Jackson Family Saga"… This epic novel is filled with emotion, mystery and love, not to mention a treasure of silver and gold. The story sweeps the reader into the lush pasturelands of Kentucky and tells a head spinning tale that will leave readers breathless. Is there really a treasure or is it a hoax?

    Book One **A BRIDGE OF DREAMS**, came out in 2018 and was awarded "Finalist," in American Book Awards in 2019. Book two, **CRYSTAL FALLS**, won the same award in 2018, And book three, **AWAKEN MY HEART**, follows in competition for the 2020 award which will be announced in August 2020.

History, romance, and a fast-paced adventure pulls you into the aura that is Christine Wissner.

Come follow her on Facebook, too:
www.facebook.com/christine.wissner.5